KEEP IN THE LIGHT

KEEP IN THE LIGHT
BOOK 1

DAVID MUSSER

ACKNOWLEDGMENTS

This book was so much fun to write, and in doing so I want to thank:

Megan Anderson - Talking online and an offhand remark that I always wanted to write a book but did not think I could write led to all this. I told her I felt I had at least one good story to tell, and I hope you agree. Thank you to Megan, the first fan of this story.

Rachel Musser – For whom I always wanted to write a wonderful story. I'm a little sorry that it had to be a horror story, but that is my brain. Thank you for always encouraging me to be the best I can be.

Lisa Musser - Thank you for all that you do and, most of all as it relates to this book, the gift of time.

Lianne Chan - I appreciate you taking the time to read and provide wonderful observations that often challenged my thinking.

Katy Madagan - Your feedback on the preface gave me the confidence to continue.

You the Reader - Thank you for taking a chance on me as a new author.

CONTENTS

PREFACE

Tommy approached the house and smiled when he saw all the lights off. What luck, this meant his mom must still be asleep. Dad's car was gone too, so it was all good. His father worked the night shift, so sneaking out after his mother took her sleeping pills was not difficult. Usually, he came home a lot earlier, but this party had been a great one.

Brushing his dark brown hair back, he thought about Lana. She had been there, and they had talked for hours about everything and nothing. What a wonderful night.

His smile faded when he walked through the door as his mother turned on the kitchen lamp. She liked the lamp at night. It was a lot easier on her eyes, he knew.

"Come on in, Tommy," she said. "Good party? You been drinking?"

"Yeah," he started, then stammered, as he sometimes did when he was nervous. "Yes, it was a good party, and no, I was not drinking, Mom. Lana was going, and I had to be there."

She sat for a while, letting him squirm until she finally said, "Sit down and shut the door."

He smiled as they eased into the familiar pattern. He knew she wasn't really mad, just worried. "But if I sit down, I can't shut the door, and if I shut the door first, then I'm not following directions… what to do what to do…," looking at the situation, he pulled the nearest chair over, sat in it, and then shut the door. "There, problem solved," he said, continuing to scooch the chair over to the table.

"Well not the only problem, mister stay up late." she started. "You know you are grounded? Only question is, how long? Did you set a date with Lana? Will her dad be upset with you for having her out late at a party?" She asked multiple questions. The way his brain worked, she knew he'd start thinking on each and the ramifications of the answers. She wasn't really mad at him. *He's been going out for a while and it's nice that he is finally making friends. They seem like good kids. Mostly a little beer from what the other parents said,* she was thinking to herself.

"I hope she does not get in trouble. She was there with her older sister, and we made a plan to meet at the movies Friday night. Can I go?" he asked.

"No, you may not meet her at the movie, you will call her tomorrow and arrange to pick her up and drive her to the movie. If it's a real date she will appreciate it and you will not keep her out longer than twenty minutes after the movie is over. Her mom and dad will appreciate that," his mom said, before tagging on, "and Saturday you will clean out the barn!"

He knew she was letting him off very easy. "Thanks, Mom," he said. "How about I make us some pancakes? Dad will be home, and we can heat them up for him."

"Sounds like a good plan, and from now on you will tell me when you are going out, or I will take those keys you are so happy to have. How was the field trip?" she asked, turning to the next subject, her warning completed.

"It was great, they had a lot of different exhibits from around the world. I think that Dad would like it. You know how his brain works," he said. She was happy to hear him excited about anything that they did in school and his acknowledgement of his father's quirkiness amused her because they both were two sides of the same coin when it came to that. *Define Problem, Fix Problem,* she thought to herself in her husband's voice.

Standing up, he hugged her, and she smelled good. He would always remember her scent that night. He would sometimes cry when he smelled it later in life. Moving over to the cabinets, he started getting everything ready and in a trick of light from the lamp, he could have sworn he saw something move across the counter.

Shaking his head, he continued to get things ready. *Almost like a hand reaching out of the darkness* he thought. It gave him a cold chill and made him remember something long forgotten.

"Mom, remember when I was sick?" he asked, and she nodded her head. He had only been ill a few times as a kid, but the "When I was sick" story was always the same one. He was seven and running a fever that reached 105 degrees before they put him in the ice-filled tub to break it. He remembered how good it felt, good and painful he always thought. How crazy it was.

"Just before the bath, Mom, do you remember what I saw?"

"How could I forget. You wore that top hat for six months after," she said.

"Ha, I'd forgotten the hat. Forgot most of it until now but could have sworn I just saw something," he said a little nervously while continuing to pour the batter into the pan for the first pancake.

About an hour before the ice bath, his father had been stalking back and forth, not knowing what to do. He was a man of action, and this sick pale boy could not be fixed by ice cream, or going hunting, or any of the life lessons he planned to teach him. Then he had an idea. "I'm going to get some ice. We can give him an ice bath, get the temperature down, and then drive to Marion," his father had said with the relief of a man who had finally found something to fix.

Grabbing his keys, his father headed out, shouting over his

shoulder, "I love you all," as he headed out to the local market for ice. "Fill up the tub, hon."

Tommy's mother stopped wiping his brow with the damp cloth and went into the bathroom. He could hear the tub starting. His teeth would not stop chattering. He didn't understand how he could be so hot according to his mother, yet still feel so cold.

Looking towards the bathroom, he saw them. Standing there. Not in the room but standing on the wall. He could barely comprehend what he was seeing but it looked exactly like a shadow of a man, and he was wearing a hat like Abraham Lincoln wore in that book he had to read last year. A top hat.

Looking at them he asked, "Who are you?" both looked at him. He could feel their eyes more than see them on him, and the power he felt from them as he started to shake.

"When your father got home with the ice, you just started with the convulsions, screaming Shadow Men, Mommy! I didn't know what to do, but your father was amazing, he dumped the ice in the tub faster than you'd ever believe he could move. Scooped you up and sat right down in the tub with you and the ice. Rubbing it over your head and shoulders, singing some lullaby that he used to sing to you when you were a baby," she added.

Tommy saw something move again. Looking down he saw it was just a shadow from the chair on the floor, but he could have sworn it moved.

His mom continued, "Don't mention that to him. It may embarrass him, but he was so sweet and wonderful holding you and—" her voice cut off as she started coughing.

Tommy looked back away from the third pancake at his mother to see she was shaking. Her hair began turning gray right in front of his eyes. She looked like she was aging. "What the fuck," he said as he turned and yanked the table away.

He could see it then, a small shadow sliding from behind the refrigerator and what could be a tentacle holding onto her ankle.

Touching the skin between her PJ bottoms and her bedroom slippers.

Pulling her to him, he turned on the kitchen light, and the shadow retreated behind the refrigerator. His mom continued to cough and shake. "Tommy?" she asked "I can't see very well. Did the light go out?"

"Mom it will be okay, I've got you," he said, pulling her toward the door. He picked up the landline and dialed 911. He got out a "help" as the operator answered before his mom started to shake again. Looking down, he saw the shadow reaching out from under the counter. His mother continued to age in front of him. Her hair had turned completely white, and her eyes had the same look as grandpa's before he passed. *Must run in the family* he thought for some stupid reason.

"RUN TOMMY! RUN!!!" she yelled, bringing him back to the moment. "Forget me and run," but he couldn't. Picking her up, she was lighter than she had been.

Moving to the center of the kitchen surrounded by light, he saw the shadow circling the room. It was sticking to the shadows, never more than an inch or two in the light. Kneeling, he cradled his mom while humming a lullaby that his father would recognize. Crying, as she passed.

He wasn't sure how long he sat there, but when he noticed the lights flicker, he could see smoke from the pancake still in the pan.

Looking at the light and then at the switch, he could see a small strip of the shadow trailing up the wall behind the phone cord to the light switch. *It's short circuiting the lights,* he thought.

Jumping up, he ran. The shadow was near the kitchen door, so the back door was the only chance. He hit the light switch as he entered the living room but could see the shadow behind him, slithering under the couch behind the chair. *I have to make the back door,* he thought but knew it was impossible. Turning, he ran down the hall, hitting the switch as he did and finally making it to his father's study.

The shadow slowed when it hit the hall but was still creeping. He could feel it and sense it. Once in the study, he flipped the light switch and turned on his father's desk lamp. *Please hurry!* he thought, unsure whether he wanted his father or the police. *How would he explain this to them?*

Sitting on the floor against a bookshelf, were all his father's mementos. An old boombox was there with a hand crank to power it, a Father's Day present a few years before from his wife. Both used to be into some weird music according to Tommy. A note from his mom propped in front read, "In Case of Emergency - ROCK!"

As time passed, he started to cry a little as he thought of his mother and watched for the shadow. Still, he must have missed when it entered the room because the desk lamp started to flicker. "Where are the cops?" he asked the air, already knowing the answer—at least another forty minutes away.

There he could see it. Under the desk at the cord, and that was smoke he was smelling in here, but not pancakes, electrical.

The Shadow was curled around the cord, swirling around and around, but stopped when Tommy uttered "Fuck you!"

It was looking at him, he did not see any eyes but Tommy knew. He in the light and it under the desk, he knew it was looking at him. "FUCK YOU!" he yelled. *Did it move back? No that could not have happened.*

"I HATE YOU! HATE YOU!" he screamed with all his might, and sure enough it moved back.

Light and sound? he wondered,. *Could it be?* "Do you feel pain?" he asked the creature that had once again started swirling around the cord, seemingly ignoring Tommy. "No, you are not ignoring me, you are trying to make me think you are," Tommy said to it.

Tommy started to sing as loud as he could. "HENERY THE EIGHTH, I AM, I AM I GOT MARRIED TO THE WIDOW NEXT DOOR SHE'S BEEN MARRIED SEVEN TIMES BEFORE AND EVERYONE WAS A HENERY." It was a silly fun song from

Herman's Hermits that he and his dad sang if the fish weren't biting before quitting. One of those stupid things parents and kids do once, that becomes a tradition. The secret language of a family.

"YOU MOVED!" he yelled at it, and it did. Then he started to laugh. "You are fucking dead," he said to the shadow. Standing, he grabbed the boombox and started to crank it, powering up the batteries. "In Case of Emergency, ROCK," he yelled as the creature shrank back under the desk.

Tommy moved in front of the office door and the creature, anticipating his escape, came out as he pressed play. It took a second but the creature following the shadow that Tommy cast on the floor touched his ankle causing such intense heat and cool that he couldn't move.

Then Tommy heard the guitar, and the drums blasting from the boombox. His mom as a joke had turned it all the way up and removed the volume knob. "I think that someone is trying to kill me, Infecting my blood and destroying my mind…" the song from Mastodon-Blood and Thunder Tommy would later find out, came blasting from the boombox and the creature shrank back under the desk, which Tommy promptly flipped over, exposing it to the light, and leaving only the shadow cast from the desk's top as a place of retreat for the creature..

"You are going to die!" Tommy yelled over the music as he pointed the boombox into that tiny spot. Holding it there as the song continued, "Break your backs and crack your oars, men, if you wish to prevail."

Looking up, Tommy could see his face in the reflection of the glass. He had a gray streak in his normally dark brown hair. The look in his eyes pleased him. *This thing would die now. It had to.* he thought.

Tommy could feel it getting weaker and growing smaller, until it finally stopped moving. It was dead. He was not sure how it was alive to begin with, but he knew it was dead.

Looking up he noticed the curtains were on fire. The door

was blocked, the bookshelf was burning "Well at least I took you with me," he said to the empty room as the window crashed inward.

His father jumped through the window and began wrapping him in a wet blanket as he pulled him into the hallway through the fiery doorway. "WHERE IS YOUR MOM?" his dad shouted.

"The kitchen. She's dead." Tommy whispered, pointing as he let the tears flow.

Moving down the hall and into the kitchen, his father bent over his wife, seeing the truth of Tommy's words for himself. Tommy could see the puzzled expression on his face as he placed two fingers on his lips and then to hers that were aged well beyond her years.

Going outside, he turned to his son. "No time now before the cops and firetrucks get here. It was an electrical fire, nothing more. I don't know what you did or what happened but say nothing." Tommy started to interrupt, and he continued "I'm not blaming you. I know this was not a simple fire son. We can talk about it later and figure it all out. Electrical fire, you smelled smoke and went to investigate and passed out." his father said to him, having to yell over the music, and it was then that Tommy realized he was still holding the boombox. The same one that would sit on every shelf in every office he would ever have.

CHAPTER 1
AFTER PARTY

"Wow that party sucked," Janet said to no one in particular as she walked down Parker's Lane toward her dorm room.

Brushing back her long dark hair, she continued her rant. "Go to college, study, make friends, and go to amazing parties." Okay, it didn't really say that in the brochure but come on. "Wow, it's exciting to drink, oh and drugs are cool. NOT!"

Janet, or Lucky as her family and friends called her, had been excited to go to this party. Jerry was going, and she had been so eager to see him and find out what he was doing before heading back home tomorrow. But he spent the evening sitting back in a recliner, a funnel in his mouth, a joint in his hand, engaging in a juvenile game with his friends who took turns pouring beer in the funnel and insisting he take a hit off the joint anytime he gagged on the beer.

Well as her mother said, "Just because a boy's pretty, doesn't make him smart or a good one."

"Give me a break," she said again and thought *Where I'm from you are finishing your father's beer for him when you mom's not looking at eleven, and many smoke their first joint with their crazy aunt and or uncle by thirteen. So, it's not a big deal. Is that it? Do people that think booze or pot are exotic make a bigger deal of it?*

She had a crazy uncle, but she did not smoke with him. He was kind of cool. He'd taught her how to shoot. Her father was an excellent shot, but even he admitted that his brother was better.

"I'm better with a shotgun. You don't have to hit a small target or center mass. I can take the top off a man at twenty feet. What else do you need?" he would say.

It would be fun to get back home for a bit. This was spring break of her freshman year. So far, other than her boyfriend situation, everything was coming up sevens. No choice of a major yet; maybe she would decide to be a nurse.

Passing Carter Hall, she felt a twinge; something was wrong. These twinges or feelings were why her parents called her Lucky. She could feel it, something was going to happen. Listening, she heard quick footsteps and turned around as Jerry almost collided with her.

"Lucky, Lucky, where are you going?" he slurred. "I wanted to see you before I go home. Gimme a hug," he demanded as he reached out for her.

"You are stupid drunk, Jerry, and I'm not in the mood!"

She stopped, looking up at a light that flickered, and felt scared. *Of him? if not then who?*

"Come on Lucky, let's get you. Get it? Get Lucky," he smiled as if she'd never heard that one before.

"F-off Jerry!" she yelled as she headed toward her dorm. She could hear him coming behind her and she knew what he was going to do. She could see it in her mind before it happened. Jerry grabbed her left shoulder to spin her around, but instead of turning, she planted her feet and grabbed his hand, turning with his momentum, and threw him. It was a simple judo throw. Nothing fancy but it worked. If anyone had been around to see it, they would have thought it a spectacular throw as Jerry went flying into the bushes beside the path.

"Bitc—" he started to say as he struggled up, but before he could she kicked him in the ass, and he went face forward into the ground.

"Stay down, Jerry!" she shouted at him.

The streetlights flickered again. *Something's wrong* she thought. "Go home, Jerry!" she yelled over her shoulder, hurrying to her room.

Inside the dorm with the lights on, she felt better. Maybe she was catching a cold. Her radar had never gone off like that before when there wasn't something…

Her mother explained it best. "Some people have a faster reaction time than others and they are more aware of their surroundings. So, what you think of as luck, or something super-natural is really just the fact that you are observant. Watch a quarterback sometime, the good ones will move when someone is about to grab them but will keep looking downfield. Is that super-" her mom had been cut off by her father yelling from somewhere in the house "It's her superpower don't mess with it."

She missed them so much right then. Entering her room, she made a quick decision - she was awake, and everything was already packed, so she grabbed her backpack and keys and headed for her jeep.

Outside once again, she noticed that the streetlight that had been flickering were completely out. Keys in hand, she reached in her backpack and pulled out her tactical flashlight. "Thirteen hundred lumens and a steel body baby, you can't get better than that," her uncle had told her when he had given it to her for her sixteenth birthday.

Turning the light on, she swept the area in front and behind her just to be sure. Nothing that she could see was out of place, but no use taking a chance. Jerry could be hiding to jump out and scare her. She couldn't wait to hear his apology on her cell when he sobered up.

Almost to the parking lot, she could just make out her jeep in the shadows. *Not far now. What is going on? One hundred yards, eighty, seventy, sixty.*

That was it, she could not take whatever was going on. She broke into a run. "F this," she said, running while moving the flashlight back and forth in one hand, and pressing the remote start for the jeep with the other. The lights turned on. Twenty feet, ten feet, "Just past this van," she said.

"Boo!" Jerry shouted as he jumped out from behind the van.

Screaming, she hit him three times in the face before she knew what she was doing. He went down to one knee.

"You broke my nose, I was just kidding, I'm sawry," he slurred the final word as he kneeled on the ground, his face in both hands.

Stepping past him, she got the jeep door open. "Lose my number!" she shouted as she tossed in the backpack, got in, and slammed the door. It was in gear and spinning gravel on Jerry as she flew out of the parking lot.

Never look back, forward always forward. If you don't move, you die. She had read this or saw it in a movie once.

She'd stop at a pharmacy, or maybe a gas station, and get some aspirin or something for her fever. That had to be it. *I must be getting sick,* she was thinking.

Never once did she look back as she headed for the interstate, wanting to put some distance between her and whatever was going on.

Behind her, still sitting on his knees in the gravel holding his face, Jerry threw up. "Fuc...bi..." he spat out between heaves.

He was sitting in the dark. "Another light out. This school is falling apart," he said aloud to the air around him.

Looking down at his hands he noticed the blood on them from his nose, and lip. Yes, his lip was cut. He could not believe it. The blood looked cool in the darkness.

She was fast! he thought. He had not planned to do anything but seeing her coming back out of the dorm he'd known where she was going and couldn't help himself.

He had made it behind the van in plenty of time. "Wow that light is bright," he remembered thinking, and it had sure hurt his eyes. Looking through the van's windows had given him the perfect view of her. He had seen her, and that weird light had made some funky shadows all around her. It was almost as if whenever she had moved the light, the shadows had moved in the opposite direction.

"Duh," he said to himself "She moved the flashlight and the shadows moved, man you are so stoned." Still, they had looked odd.

Standing he forgot completely about the shadows and Lucky, taking off his T-shirt to use it to stop the bleeding before wiping his mouth. He lay back with his head against the van. If he had opened his eyes, he would have noticed the shadows swirling around in the sky above him. Two of them were swirling in circles, one dipping, while the other circled it. A sportsman would have seen them as two predators fighting over prey, but Jerry was no sportsman, and he was dead before Lucky hit the interstate.

They would find him the next day, or what was left of him. Spontaneous human combustion would be the listed cause of death. Nothing but ash inside of his clothes.

Lucky felt better when she hit the interstate. Giggling to herself a little. She had never really hit someone before. Sure, she had during martial arts practice but never in reality. Her hand didn't even hurt. Did she hit him with the flashlight hand or the key hand? She couldn't remember at first, then remembered it was two with the key hand and the final one with the flashlight. Curled in her fist like that it was better than the roll of dimes she always carried in her backpack.

"Being paranoid pays off every time," she said and laughed as she turned on the radio.

"And tonight, on Coas—" it started as she changed the station "President says no nee—" She changed the station again and found nothing she felt like listening to, so she plugged her phone in and fired up her favorite playlist.

Relaxing finally, she looked around and laughed at what she discovered. When had she done it? She didn't know, but the dome light was on. *What, was she afraid of the dark now? Wow big college girl.*

She turned off the dome light and relaxed into the drive. It was too late to call her parents to let them know she was coming home, but she was glad to be on the way.

Letting her mind wander, she thought of home and her wonderful father, who was only slightly less paranoid than his brother. How they even left the house each day with worrying about what would happen when they were gone was a mystery. She knew that if her uncle had been her father instead, he'd never have agreed to letting her go to college ten hours away from him. He would have moved.

Her father in fact had mentioned moving with her several times, but thankfully her mom had realized she needed to get out and experience the real world.

"Our home is not like the rest of the world. People here, aside from your father and uncle, still don't lock their doors at night, and some let the cars run while running into a store for something quickly in the winter. You will meet some amazing people and some ass-hats. You just have to figure out which are which," her mother had warned her as she was packing for the trip.

Her father had been less verbal about his love for her or his desire to see her protected. Instead, on her last day home, he'd spent several hours in his workshop. She thought that he was sulking, and maybe he was a little, but when she went to get him for lunch, he had handed her the backpack.

"It's heavy, but you are strong. I made it out of a bullet resistant material and placed a couple steel plates in there that can be removed. There is also a side compartment for a flashlight and the lining can be pulled back to hide a knife or gun there. Unless someone knows what they are looking for or it's X-rayed without the plates in it, no one will know you are packing," he'd said evenly.

She hugged him. He was paranoid but trying. "I love it, Daddy, I'll carry it everywhere," and she had.

Pulling into the gas station, she wished she was packing a gun but she only had a small knife, and of course the flashlight. Grabbing her backpack off the seat, she put it on her shoulder, paid for the gas at the pump, and filled up.

Tony noticed the jeep pull in under the lights. Through the glass it cast an odd shadow behind it. Almost a double shadow. *Very odd* he thought.

Figuring this was just another gas and go, he turned to the sunglass mirror on the counter. Looking for which pair would accidentally disappear on his shift, he noticed a pimple that was just ready to go.

He decided to pop it, which spewed blood and pus on the small mirror. Wiping his face, he noticed the lights of the jeep brighten the store.

Just after filling the tank, Lucky pulled into the front of the store, and then, remembering her uncle's admonishment to always back in, she quickly whipped it around and backed into the spot instead.

Tony saw the woman swinging the jeep around and muttered, "Crazy Driver," and then, louder, "WOW," as he saw Lucky get out. She looked stunning in the light. Self-consciously he wiped his chin to make sure the blood was gone.

In the station, the TV was on, showing one of the news stations talking about some asteroid that would be closer to the earth than any in a hundred years. The screen panned to show people standing around with signs protesting everything imaginable. Some had signs proclaiming, "The end is upon us!"

Grabbing aspirin, snacks, and a bottle of water, Lucky paid the young man, thanked him, and headed out to the jeep. *He's kind of cute,* she thought as she started the jeep. Pulling out, she could have sworn that the lights behind her in the station blinked, but that must be her imagination. She turned up the radio and headed back to the interstate.

Inside the store, Tony watched her drive away, wishing he would have had the courage to say more than the "nice jeep," that he'd managed to get out. The lights blinked, but the store was crap, so he was not surprised, only glad they came back on.

"Stupid. Stupid. Stupid!" he said, scolding himself. *Oh well, shift will be over soon,* he thought.

He picked up the clipboard and looked at the things left to do. He checked off a couple that no one would be able to tell, then laughing said "Oh a pair of sunglasses was stolen," before picking out the pair he liked and wiping off the little bit of pimple pus that was on them, before placing them in his pocket.

Starting to whistle, he picked up the trashcan from behind the counter, and a big black trash bag off the shelf under the register, dropping the smaller bag in, and moving around the store, whistling while he worked.

Moving outside, he went into the restrooms, emptying the trash cans into the bag. It was a good night, nothing too gross in the stalls.

When he walked towards the dumpster, he saw some dude standing in front of it. "Hey man—" he started and waved, a little scared, but it wasn't a man. It was his own shadow. Looked different. Standing there he moved his head back and forth and the shadow mimicked him. "Yup that's me. Never been scared by my own shadow before," he said aloud, his voice cracking ever so slightly.

Picking up the bag again that he had dropped when he startled himself, he walked toward the dumpster. Inside, he felt that something was wrong. Looking around he called out, "Anyone there?"

There was no response. He opened the side door to the dumpster, his shadow still watching him. *Makes me look like I have a hat on* he thought.

He tossed the bag, but it didn't go all the way in. Pushing it in, holding the door ready to close it, he noticed all at once how dark it was inside the dumpster, and that his hand was going numb when it touched the darkness. Tony was frozen in fear beside the dumpster as the Shadow fed.

Though Lucky had taken the aspirin immediately, it wasn't until a few hours later as she drove into the sunrise that she began to feel better. Pulling off to the side of the road, she climbed out to stretch and take the top down.

"Gonna be a good day!" she told the sun.

CHAPTER 2
CHORES

Kane loved living on the farm. The fresh air every morning, and the feeling of accomplishment at the end of each day. There was nothing better. Mama had wanted him to go away to college after he graduated high school but since he did not want to do anything other than farm, and hiring a hand would cost more than the farm made, he decided to work the farm in the morning and take night classes at the local community college.

Kane's father had died several years before of cancer. "Sometimes the brightest candles burn the fastest," his mother would say, just before reminding him of all that his father had built. Starting with nothing, moving to a strange area after his service in the military, marrying the farmer's daughter he'd met while working for her father the summer before. He had planned to move on to LA. He was a big man with dark hair, and he'd figured he'd find work as a movie extra, maybe play the heavy. Everyone said that Kane looked so much like him.

His father never really had a plan for life, he had just let it unfold. He'd gone into the Marines because his parents had asked him on his eighteenth birthday when he was moving out.

They had not offered to help get a loan for school or anything, just expected him to be gone.

He packed a small bag, joined the service, and eight years later he'd had enough. He loved it and loved everyone he worked with. They felt like family, but some of the changes in leadership had them doing stuff he did not fully understand.

Checking out, he'd been traveling west, and when he was just south of Marion, hitchhiking as one could do back then, he'd encountered a farmer with a truck full of hay bales. They weren't the round bales of today, but the old square bales. The driver had offered a meal and a place to stay for the night if he would help him unload the truck.

Grandpa Milner had one farm and a few off-site fields that he used for hay, and that morning his old hand had quit; he wanted to be a welder. So, Grandpa picked up the hitchhiker, had taken him home to unload the hay, and as the story goes, he'd married the farmer's daughter.

His father had passed away when Kane was twelve. It had been a horrible few months, and Kane would have dropped out of school completely if not for his father's admonishment. "An uneducated man is beholden to others – so get an education and then you can decide what you want to do."

Kane loved being a farmer and working with his hands; he had to remind himself of that. He loved every minute of it, except cleaning out the hog pens. There was no good way to do this, at least on his budget. He had to hurry but knew if he did not do it right, he'd just have to clean it earlier the next time.

Later, when he was finished, he looked at the hogs and told them they would just have to wait for their slop, he was going to clean up and get lunch. Walking towards the house he thought *Not bad, a full day's work done in half.*

Going inside he heard his mom yelling at Grandpa Milner. Not really mad it sounded like, but something had set her off, and she was fuming as she entered the kitchen.

"Why did you show him that channel?" she asked.

Playing dumb he asked, "What channel, Ma?"

"You know the one, the all-day all-night yoga channel. Every time I take something to his room, he has it on. You are going to give that man a heart attack. He is just as ornery as you. Your father was the same way. I don't know how I survived having you three around," she said while moving to the fridge to start making him lunch.

She kept fuming even as he turned his back. Heading upstairs to clean up, he made sure to hide the smile on his face. He had told Grandpa to turn it off or change the channel if she was around. *Old Coot will get us both beds in the barn*, he thought.

It felt odd taking a shower and cleaning up this early. Reminded him of when he was in school, doing half between four and eight a.m. and the rest after school, but today was different. Janet was coming home.

He wondered if she'd changed much or if she would be the same. Wished he had told her all those years they lived beside each other how he felt but she was destined for better things.

She's lucky like that, he thought and laughed, thinking about how everyone, even her parents, called her Lucky. He refused to, though. He called her by her proper name because to him a name was special.

Downstairs, his mom was finishing putting lunch on the table and she asked with a knowing smile. "Got plans today? I noticed you were up early."

"I'm helping Mr. Evans today," he started as he took a bite of the turkey sandwich and chewing said, "He's getting ready for Janet's birthday party. She's coming home today."

"I had no idea," she lied and continued to kid him and grill him, but in that sweet mom way she had, and he knew that she would be as happy as he was if Lucky and he ever became more. They had practically never left each other's side until she went to college. If not for her tutoring while he worked the farm at night, he would never have graduated.

He wanted to tell her a hundred times, or more, how he felt

but wondered if it was fair to her. To make her a farmer's wife. It was not as glamorous a life as she was destined for, but he was going to tell her. No matter what, during this trip home for her, he was going to talk to her and profess his love. That is, unless she'd met some college boy, a football player, or some pretty boy.

Just then his mother smacked him on the back of his head. "Get out of your own head, Kane, just talk to her and things will work out as they will, okay?"

"Okay, Ma, thank you," he said while finishing. Rising and kissing the top of her head on his way out he said, "Sorry about Grandpa. I told him not to let you see what he was watching," laughing as he ran for the door. She threw her dish towel at him, cursing as he headed for his truck. She loved seeing him drive his father's old GMC Sierra.

Kane pulled up to the house and could see Mr. Evans filling up the tractor. He already had the mower blades on it. Parking he got out and asked, "Need a hand today, Mr. Evans?"

Mr. Evans stood up and seemed to frown a little before smiling at Kane. Mr. Evans was one of the few people around bigger than Kane. Kane stood at six foot three, and two-ninety. Mr. Evans must have been six foot six and a good three-fifty. It hadn't happened yet, that he knew of anyway, but Kane did not want to get on Mr. Evans' bad side.

"Always, Kane, but today especially. Lucky's getting home today. I need to get ready for the party. Your ma and grandpa coming?" he asked.

"Ma said she is and that she will check with Mrs. Evans on what to bring, and you know Grandpa. He would not miss a party if women are gonna be there" he said, laughing again. He noticed the frown on Mr. Evans face... *Did he know?* but it passed.

Should he ask her dad's permission to ask her out? I should ask Janet, he thought, realizing though he always used her as a sounding board for most life questions, he couldn't ask her this.

"You start mowing down the drive and by the road. Don't

want any of our cousins missing that turn again," Mr. Evans said.

"Great! I'll take care of it, sir," he said, throwing the sir for good measure as he took off his shirt and tied it around his waist before hopping on the tractor.

Mr. Joe Evans wiped his hands on his pants and headed inside. Opening the door, he saw his wife Kate holding out her hand.

"I told you he'd be here before one o'clock. Pay up, mister," she said.

Reaching into his pocket, he pulled out his wallet, handed her a twenty, and said, "Damn boy even called me sir. I don't know if she's ready for what he's going to say, and I had hoped he would wait until she was done college."

"They are the only two that don't know how the other feels. It's funny and sad. He's a good man, and she could do way worse," Kate said.

"Ginger's mom told me that Ginger had moved some of her classes at the community college to night classes just to be near Kane. But while he was friendly enough, he only talked to her about Lucky, well about Janet. It really upsets Ginger that he is the only one allowed to call her by her given name without getting a punch in the arm. Even us," and they both laughed as they shared one of those wonderful parent moments.

"It's cute," Kate said, smiling, and then went on to tell him all the things he still had to take care of before the party that weekend. Kate was a natural planner which was only one of the things he loved about her.

Kane had been mowing for a while and was almost done, when he heard Janet's jeep take the turn to come down the lane. She was behind him, so he stopped and turned around.

Lucky saw him and could not believe how good he looked; she bit her lower lip wondering why they never became more as she pulled to a stop beside him. Climbing out of the jeep while he got off the tractor, she took two last quick steps and wrapped her arms around him. She wasn't sure why, but she needed to feel his arms around her as she whispered, "Keep me safe."

"Always," he said. He had said this to her a thousand times over the years. From the first time that she'd tried riding a bull in the local rodeo to the first time she'd driven her father's tractor. It had been without permission of course, but Kane had taught her, and her father had been pleasantly surprised to find the yard mowed when he got home.

Kane wasn't sure how long they stayed like that. He kept holding her and in the back of his mind he was glad Mr. Evans did not have any cameras here. Mr. Evans was not your average farmer. He placed a lot of faith in technology. Cameras at every entrance and even on the river that passed through the lower pasture. He wanted to know when anyone was on his property. Even had magnetic sensors in the driveway to detect vehicles.

As Kane thought of this, Lucky was just thinking how warm and good it felt in Kane's arms. She could smell the same after-shave that she had given him every year for Christmas since he started shaving. It was her favorite scent.

The magnetic sensors Kane thought as he heard Mr. Evan's truck coming up the lane. There was no time to say all he wanted to say so he kissed her on top of the head and said, just loud enough for her to hear "Janet, I love you."

She shook a little at hearing this. She had always known deep down, *but why now?* She wondered if he could sense something was wrong. *Damn him, I'm not ready for him. I may never be ready for him. I need this like I need a hole in the head right now, but what if…What if he's the reason all other boys are just that, boys. Damn him, I wish I could talk to him about this,* she thought, realizing he's the one that always helped her talk through things.

Hearing her father's truck, she pulled back out of his arms. No need to give her father a heart attack. *Yet another boy to worry about, right, Dad?* she thought and then, without thinking, she strained to her tip toes to kiss Kane quickly on the lips, telling him as she stepped back, "We need to talk, you ass-hat." Then for good measure, she punched him in the arm and said, "Call me Lucky."

Stepping back while acting like a wounded puppy, he turned, smiled, and said, "Never, Janet, you will never be that lucky," then laughed loud and hard, and Lucky felt safe. She was home.

Now what to tell Mom she thought.

She hugged her father who had just gotten out of the truck. Seeing Kane back on the tractor looking at Janet, his little girl, he joked, "The help has not been bugging you have they ma'am."

He kept himself from frowning as he noticed her cheeks blush just a little. *Damn him*, he thought. *I hope she's ready.*

They took her jeep back to the house. He knew that Kane would bring the truck. *We will never get rid of that boy now, Well, we could do worse*, he thought.

"So how long you out of the joint for?" he asked.

"Daaad," she said, emphasizing the a's. "I'm on spring break and it's college, not jail. It was wonderful thank you for asking." Then as she saw the sad look on his face, said, "I missed you and Mom a ton, Dad, but I have to be out on my own and have my own experiences. You know that."

"I know, Lucky. Just so glad you are home. I had a nightmare last night," he said and if he'd been looking at her instead of driving, he would have noticed her shake.

Parking the jeep, he said "I love driving your jeep," then yelled into the house "Ma'am we have another boarder. Hope this one is better than the last," then to his daughter he said, "I love you, honey. I'm glad you are home. I'll get the bags, you go catch up with your mom."

Kate came out to give Lucky a giant hug, and holding hands, they went into the kitchen, stopping to hold the door open for Joe.

Inside, as he crossed the room, her father said over his shoulder, "She kissed Kane," and Lucky's jaw dropped, her face turning beet red. She turned and punched her father in the arm harder than she had hit Kane. Her father laughed but stopped when he saw Lucky holding her hand.

"I'm sorry, Lucky, I knew you were gonna tell your Mom. I didn't mean for you to hurt yourself hitting me." he said while looking at her hand.

"I did not hurt it hitting you," she said, happy to change the conversation from kissing Kane. *How had he seen anyway? Or did he guess?* He cheated. He guessed. He had the same luck as she did. For him it was more for daily things, like knowing when to fill in a hole before a cow would step in it or knowing when to take down a tree before it would fall, but it was the same type of thing.

"I got in a fight last night. Got to use my Judo!" she laughed. "Threw the boy over my shoulder into the bushes and broke his nose when I hit him."

Her father stopped moving, holding her hand as he did, looking at her wrist as he said slowly, "Who is he, where does he live?"

The coolness in his voice scared her, not for herself but for whoever would really hurt her. The unsaid "and do I need to kill him" said more than he could ever say about how much he loved her. "It's okay, Daddy. I handled it. I'm not a little girl anymore," she said and wished she hadn't. "I'm sorry, seriously, it is okay, he got a little handsy and after I flipped him, he came back up like he was going to do something, and I hit him just to emphasize how much I was not into him. It is okay," she said. Not telling the entire story, or anything about what she felt that night, not wanting to worry him.

"Ouch, that hurts," she said. "Is it broken?"

"No not broke, get me the light, Kate," he said as he turned it over.

"What is this smudge here?" he asked as Kate handed him a light. Thinking it was a bad bruise on the surface he shined the light on it, fifty million lumens or whatever. *Must have imagined it* he thought, *or a trick of the eyes, it seemed to dissolve when the light hit it.*

A few minutes before, miles away, two circling shadows were joined by another larger one. They were in the trees, under the bridges, and behind rocks, always keeping to the shadows, slithering, and circling, intertwining together, and then they just stopped. If they had been sharks it would have been as if the blood in the water was gone, and like sharks they separated, waiting for that next kill. Passing different houses. Maybe enter this house? Maybe your house?

CHAPTER 3
INTERLUDE

nside a small room made of plastic, situated inside another larger room so that bright lights pointed at it from all sides, including the floor of the tiny room, the witness sat, hands shaking, as he asked "Maybe enter this house? Maybe your house?" looking up at the man standing beside him.

The man was clean shaven, on his face and head and wearing a white suit. He was visibly shaken. Looking down at the witness he cracked him across the back with his heavy duty five cell flashlight, driving the witness's head forward onto the makeshift table.

"Okay, okay I'm sorry," offered the witness. "But it's true. They could be anyplace, well not here but damned near anyplace else."

The man in white looked at the witness in disgust. *Of all that could have survived, why him?*

"Tell me again how you know all of this? How you know the intimate details of what Lucky was thinking?" he asked.

"I was their, man; I remember it all. It's a gift or a curse, but what I did not see I was told, and it's easy to figure out the rest," he continued.

"Told by wh—" the man in white started to ask as he was interrupted by the witness.

"Now, where was I? Was it Thursday or Friday? Okay, I remember. The rest of that week was so full of the typical young love stuff that you would think that neither of them had been with anyone before. They were both so careful, neither realizing how little time they had before things would go to shit. I guess my part starts after the party when Lucky visited her friend Ginger. That morning. Lucky looked so good. Did I tell you that? I was there wasn't I? Please tell me I was." The witness said shaking with hunger.

Finished talking and started to scratch his arms. Looking all around him, he saw nothing but light.

His arms were covered in scratches that looked like needle marks. He looked up with his black eyes and asked, "Can I get something to eat?"

The man in the white suit looked at the clock on the wall outside the plastic room. *No shadows, so no wearing a watch. Even a tiny watchband could hide a shadow* he thought and said, "Sure. It's time."

Leaving the room, the technician came in to administer his meds. "Fuck he is on enough to knock out a rhino, how the heck does he need more," he whispered as they pass.

That was something the man in white would have to consider. This entire thing did not make sense. When he had been given this job, there had been a few unorthodox rules to follow.

1. Wear white at all times. When working, your suit, shoes, socks, absolutely everything must be white at all times. Try to wear white all other times as well when off the clock. It is for your own safety.
2. Keep your pants and shirts tight at the extremities.
3. Never talk about the Shadows outside of the white rooms. Do not mention them in passing, do not

mention them to family or friends, and gag yourself at night if you talk in your sleep.

4. Sleep with the lights on.
5. Most importantly never notice them. Do not look at the shadows if you think you see something.

The last rule was the kicker for him. He was paid to notice things and to be able to find what was needed. That was his expertise. It was how he found the witness smashed out of his mind in that flop house. How the guy had survived was still a question. He'd gone from just below Marion to a flop house in New York without any clear path.

When he'd been hired his boss had told him, "Whatever you do, do NOT notice them. As long as you do not notice them, they will not notice you, at least that's our working assumption."

What a strange creature, he thought *the shark analogy is not far off. If you jump in the ocean at any point you are most likely not going to see a shark, but if there is blood in the water you can bet you will soon see a shark.*

"I need a drink," he said to no one as he headed for the exit. The witness would be out for hours and no good really until tomorrow. He seemed to be more lucid in the mornings.

CHAPTER 4
STALK MUCH?

Lucky had such a wonderful end to the week. Her party went off without too many issues. She was surprised that Jerry had never called her to apologize for his stupidity when he was drunk, but glad she did not have to talk to him again. *Guess he lost my number*, she thought and laughed.

When it comes to family parties there would always be stress factors to consider and plan for. *Would uncle whomever sit near his ex who is now married to cousin someone. Would everyone stare at aunt such and such with her nice new front end, as Grandpa Milner would say?*

Thankfully, everyone had been on their best behavior, even Grandpa, and her mom had been simply amazing. She could feed an army if needed.

Kane's mom was still peeved with him over showing Grandpa that channel, but it made for some interesting conversations with others of the older generation who had no idea such wonderful programming was on TV.

The night after, Lucky lay tossing and turning in the bed, before being awoken by her own screams as she fell to the floor. She had been crossing a bridge in her dream, and for some reason, had jumped into the darkness and just kept falling for what seemed like forever.

Lying on the floor, she took stock of her body and found nothing seemed the worse for the fall. Her wrist had finally started feeling better yesterday, and she was glad she had not hurt it again. She let out a sigh of relief as her door burst open.

Laughing, she looked up at her father. "Bad dream is all, Daddy. I just fell out of the bed."

Looking confused for a second, still searching for danger, her father finally placed his Smith & Wesson nine millimeter on the dresser, then bending, scooped her and her covers off the floor, and laid her on the bed. He gently kissed her on top of the head. "Scared the shit out of me, darlin'. I have not been sleeping well tonight myself," he whispered as he sat beside her on the bed.

There it is again, she thought that connection between us. *Mom never mentions it, but there was something instinctual they shared. Their superpower.*

"What's up?" he asked while rubbing her arms gently.

With a shaky voice she replied "I don't know, Daddy. Everything has been so good the last couple of weeks. I just feel like the other shoe is about to drop."

"Lay down, I'll stay 'til you are asleep," he said, moving over to the rocking chair that had been his mother's, and her mother's before. The one that had rocked him to sleep when he was a baby and someday would rock her kids to sleep.

Lying there, Lucky tried to go to sleep. She felt so safe with him in the room, she felt the chair rocking, could feel the rhythm. *I must remember to tell him about the bridge,* she thought as she finally fell asleep.

She woke up when he left the room; the old house had creaky floors. After he left, she glanced at the clock, seeing it was still a couple of hours before daybreak. She knew he would be in work mode. She thought about how much she loved Kane, realizing their life together would be very much like this one and she wondered if she was capable of being a farmer's wife. She knew how rewarding it could be, but everyone kept telling her she was destined for bigger things than this town. *Stop the deep thinking* she thought, scolding herself.

Lucky got out of bed, pulling her hair back, and dressing quickly before hurrying quietly down the steps.

She could hear him getting dressed in his office, trying to not wake her mom who would make him breakfast most mornings, though he would not allow her to do so on Saturdays or Sundays. It was a tradition started when first married. "You need your rest," he would say to her, and most of the time he would be quiet enough so that even if he woke her, she would be able to go back to sleep.

He smelled the bacon as he came down the steps and smiled at Lucky. "Thank you, dear. Are you wanting to hang out with the old man today?" he asked.

"Maybe for a bit. What's up today? I don't have to be at Ginger's until two," she said while placing his plate on the table.

They talked a lot that morning while she spent the rest of it helping him. It had been a long time since she had spent a day outside doing this type of work, and it felt good.

After lunch, Lucky helped her mom for a bit and then headed over to Ginger's. They had grown apart and she was still a little peeved with Ginger over Kane, but with only few days left before she had to head back to college, she did not want to leave things strained between them. She had been at the party, but there had been no alone time to just be together.

Ginger smiled when she heard Lucky pull up in her jeep. Ginger realized how much she missed Lucky and wondered if maybe that was her real attraction to Kane – maybe she'd just wanted her friend back. *Who knows*, she thought.

Lucky smiled when she saw Ginger at the door, and all was right with the world. They could not be more different. Ginger's blonde hair and her dark hair. One an introvert, the other an extrovert, but they had been friends forever. Inside they grabbed the pool bag, towels, and drinks that Ginger had waiting.

They headed out back to the pool as they had hundreds of times, found the best direction of the sun for tanning, and relaxed. It was something they always did well together. No talking needed, just two friends being there. Talking a little, but mainly just soaking up the sun.

Later, after a short nap, feeling a little toasty, Lucky stood up, preparing to dive into the pool, when she felt someone watching her, then saw a curtain drop upstairs. Instinctively covering herself, she yelled, louder than she meant to, "Ginger who's home?"

Ginger opened her eyes, looked at Lucky, and then looking at the same window, yelled, "That pervert I've told him a thousand times to not gawk at my friends. He's always crushed on you but still!" as she got up and began moving toward the house.

"Roy's home? I thought he was still in boot camp?" Lucky asked, following her inside and up the steps, having to run to keep up.

Roy's door was at the end of the hall, and as they approached Lucky saw a big "KEEP OUT" sign on it, and a couple playbills from some bands that Roy had seen in New York. Nothing that would ever be played on the radio or on any of the music services she was sure. There were a couple of symbols, some demonic, from movies, and some she thought of from that popular children's book about warlocks. "He'll never grow up," she thought as she shivered from the air conditioner in the house.

The door was locked, so Ginger started banging on it while cursing her brother. "I've told you to leave my friends alone," she yelled and continued to yell different half sentences, the language of siblings, Lucky guessed.

"Remember Julie, Gonna tell Dad? Bust your ass, Is that pot? Open this now," she spats out, as she continued to bang on the door.

Lucky was surprised at how long Ginger kept banging on the door and cursing. She finally stopped but not before whispering into the door "I will hurt you," and Lucky knew she could too. Although Ginger was the younger, she had a mean streak in her and could always best him when fighting, as kids do. Lucky had wondered when he joined the Army, whether he was going to be tough enough.

The hall was quiet. Ginger looked back at Lucky and apologized. "I'm sorry, he moved back just after you left, and when he's not looking at my friends, he's watching his 'special web sites,'" she yelled, banging on the door again.

Frowning, she continued "Mom's not sure what to do with him, and Dad is just heartbroken. He had been so happy when Roy joined the service. The only thing Dad loved more than the service was the TV show he named us after. Luckily for him he wasn't named after the title."

"It's okay," Lucky said. "What happened with the service?"

"Pot, heroin, drugs of some sort, probably jerking off in the shower to the other men," she yelled back at the door and banged on it a few more times.

On the other side of the door, Lucky could see a shadow of movement and then came a banging on the other side of the door. Mocking Ginger, she felt.

The banging kept going until finally Ginger said "F-it, let's get out of here."

Turning to leave, Lucky had another twinge that something was wrong, another chill. *It's only the AC*, she told herself.

"You are right, let's go see what Kane's doing then head to the movies," she exclaimed with an enthusiasm that seemed strained even to herself.

Roy was sitting against the door, shirt off, and pants down around his ankles. On the desk his laptop was indeed opened to one of his special sites. He sat unblinking as the creatures slowly devoured him.

Roy had been spying on Lucky. He could not help it. He liked to people watch. It made him feel something. Feel more maybe, but it had gotten him into trouble before and this time was no different.

It had gotten him drummed out of the service. The men's and women's showers had been just too close together and *BAM* like that, he'd had the shit beat out of him by some half-naked redhead and he was kicked out of the service.

Last night his watching had led to his death. He had been over at Mrs. Johnson's.. She had been Roy's English teacher in high school and was recently divorced.

He hadn't been sure why he'd gone there. Always lying to himself…. Parking down the street so she did not hear his bike, he had walked toward the house. He had started to go up and knock on the door. Like one of those movies where the conquering hero returns, but then he saw the bushes. The darkness seemed to invite him.

He had seen her in the light of her kitchen, just walking to the fridge wearing a T-shirt too large for her with only panties underneath. Roy had planned on watching her more and was just going to lower his pants but then noticed something in the darkness. *Is that a snake?* he thought at first. Then it coiled around his ankle and when it touched his skin the shock ran through him. Scared him so bad he'd farted and he knew he would have to throw away his underwear.

Running out of the bushes, hoping she would not see him, he had jumped on his bike, and headed straight home.

In his room he'd fallen asleep. Even though it hadn't been late, he was so very tired, so he had only been up for a little while when he had heard his sister and Lucky by the pool.

Lucky had grown up he had thought. *I should go down and, say hi,* but instead he'd pulled down his pants and opened the curtain more so he could get a better view. The light spilled into the room, and he turned as something darted into a corner. "Was that a fucking rat?" he asked the empty room.

He had turned, dropping the curtain, and grabbing his pellet gun. "You gonna die. I hate rats," he'd said with just a slight shake in his voice. He had forgotten about his pants and so he fell as he stepped forward. Hitting the ground, he saw the shadows move. "What the—" he'd started as the first one touched his bare legs, making them instantly go numb. Pulling himself with his arms toward the door, he'd heard the back door to the house slam shut, and Ginger yelling. *I'm saved,* he'd thought, moving closer to the door, turning around to see where it was, before noticing another.

How many rats are there? he thought, raising his pellet gun, and shooting at movement. The pellet went right through it, but his frightened mind registered a direct hit.

He'd fired again and again, the only sound was the little release of air, as the pellets passed harmlessly through the shadows.

He'd tried to scream just as Ginger hit the door the first time, but it was too late. His last thought was how much he wished he had changed his underwear from last night as the shadows continued to feed.

Outside, Ginger was apologizing to Lucky again as she flipped off her brother's window. She thought she'd seen him standing behind the curtain. Peering out. "Little creep," she yelled back to the window.

They both got in Lucky's jeep. The top was down, so Lucky reached into the dash and pulled out two scrunchies. "With our long hair we will be dead before we get to the farm," she joked, but it felt flat to her.

She was being watched again, and it did not feel like it was Roy. Felt more like when she had been escaping the school parking lot. She felt a chill go through her and started rubbing her wrist. It was hurting again.

Kane looked up from the tractor and waved as they pulled into his driveway. Yelling to him, Lucky said "We are gonna go hang with your ma, and when you are done you get to take us to the movies."

"Ain't you a lucky boy," Ginger added as both blew him kisses.

CHAPTER 5
AFRAID OF THE DARK?

Mary and Phil were just arriving home about seven from dinner with his boss's family. Phil had been with the company for a while. "A geologist by trade and a lover of life," was how Phil always described himself to others. When talking to just his wife, he would say a lover of… and after pausing would name something about her anatomy. When drinking it would sometimes be crude; and tonight, it was. She was proud of her body but wished he would show a little class.

Mary loved him, but he had changed a lot when Roy came back home. Ginger and Roy were his pride and joy. He sang that show's theme to them every time he rocked them to sleep and if possible, he loved them more than she did. Or really, he was more invested in their success. She just wanted them to be happy and healthy. She didn't care what they did. *He's a good man, just a little lost* she thought, knowing he was thinking about how to get her to bed early.

Opening the door for her, he slurred his words a bit. She had driven home. Thankfully, he always let her, handing her the keys, or trying to tuck them down her shirt when heading for the car so she would have to fumble with her top getting them out while he watched, hoping for a little peep. *Ever the teenager* she would often scold.

Ginger had texted her earlier in the day about Roy, and she had not mentioned it to Phil. He was under a lot of pressure. Possible cutbacks at work, so best to talk about that tomorrow. She saw Roy's bike on the side of the house, one of those on-off road bikes that were street legal. Mary also saw the house lights were off.

"Madam, your bed awaits," Phil slurred, taking her arm in his and walking toward the house. He tripped over something that was not there and cursed *Why didn't they leave a light on for us when they left?*

Opening the front door, he tried to spin her so that he could pin her against the door to kiss her, but he fumbled a bit. She still kissed him. God help her she loved him, but she knew it was going to be a bad night, and a bad day to follow after he heard about Roy peeping at Lucky.

Flipping the light switch and getting nothing, he flipped it a couple more times before declaring, "Breaker's off I guess. Wait here. I'll take care of it."

"Should you maybe let me?" she asked, not wanting him to electrocute himself.

"I've got it, my dear. I ain't scared of nothing in the dark," he said, giving a little bow and quickly turning for the basement.

Standing at the door, she pulled out her cell phone, turning on the flashlight option so that she could light his way. "Turn that off," he shouted. "You'll ruin my night vision," he finished, slurring just a little.

She obliged and a second later heard him bang his knee into the table beside the basement door. He grunted, and she heard him curse as he headed down the stairs.

Mary had always been a little afraid of the dark, and he had even picked on her a few times when first married, but he loved her, so like any good husband, he found night lights that would come on after dark and quit teasing her about it. Until times that he was drunk, and it did sting her a bit. "Serve him right if he falls and breaks his neck," she mumbled and was about to close the door to the outside but thought better of it as it did give a little light, so she decided to leave it open even though there was a chill outside that she could feel.

Walking down the stairs, Phil put his hand on the wall and, holding the banister, wondered how much he'd had to drink. *Did he finish that bottle?* Making it to the basement he decided to do it old school and, keeping his hand on the wall so that it didn't move, started making his way around the basement. Sure, he could have just walked straight across to the breaker box on the opposite wall, but who knows what those kids left on the floor and this way he would not fall.

Never once did he consider getting out his cell phone for the flashlight. If he had he may have seen what was in front of him. Better for him that he did not.

Reaching the breaker box, he opened it and, like his father had taught him turned off all the smaller breaker switches, then felt for the main; it was on. *Must be the power company* he thought.

He turned off the main breaker and reached down, searching for the switch to the little gas-powered electric generator. You can't live in the country without one, he thought. Flipping the switch, the engine came to life and all the little dials and switches lit up.

Something moved in the darkness. "Rats you better look out, if I sees ya I shoot ya," he said sounding a lot like Roy. He flipped over the switch to put the house on the generator. "You got two seconds to vacate," he said again, voice slurring, and a little nervous.

Giving it almost enough time, he slipped on a couple of the small breakers. He wasn't sure which one was for the basement.

Nothing happened after the first couple that he could see, but he could hear the freezer in the corner cut on. He could tell it was drawing more power from the generator from the noise it was making, being under more load. He flipped another couple more on.

He had his fingers on the next breaker, the one that would show him what had been watching him, hungering for him, what had been waiting to devour him, when he stopped, fingers still on the switch as he heard his wife scream from upstairs.

Letting go of the breaker, he turned and ran for the stairs. He could see a little light then, *one of the switches must have cut on the lights upstairs*, he thought.

Seeing movement, he did not think twice about it. Mary was in danger, he heard her scream again, and this one was cut off.

If he had looked over his shoulder, In the light from the generator, he would have seen it. He would not have been saved, but he would have known why Mary screamed.

"What the—" Phil said, looking around and stopping, turning, and turning. "Could have sworn," he said to no one. He turned back toward the stairs and the darkness was all around them. "It looks like I'm walking into an open mouth. Even has teeth," he laughed, not knowing the creature passed him as he was spinning in circles.

Phil headed for the stairs and as the darkness closed around him, he screamed, dying, never knowing what was consuming him.

When Phil had started turning on the breakers, Mary had shut the front door. She could see the hall light upstairs turn on, then a light in the kitchen, and then the lamp beside the door. "Wow they must have had them all on," she scolded the air.

She had felt something was wrong before she'd seen it. Looking around, she worried it could be something electrical. If it was not good old P-Ed's fault, there could be something wrong in the house that had caused the breakers to turn off.

Having moved just a few feet into the house, she hadn't been able to see anything. She'd heard the hum of the generator downstairs, and the fridge kick on, but something was wrong. "Roy?" she called out, sensing someone watching her.

"Roy, I'll beat you silly if you jump out at me," she said, meaning every word of it.

She looked in front of her and could not shake the feeling. "I'm out of here," she said to the air. *I've seen enough scary movies* she thought. "If something wants me, it can chase me," she said aloud, turning toward the door.

She wasn't really thinking anything was there other than the darkness, but fearing the dark had caused her a lot of jumps and gray hairs in her life. *Thank goodness for blonde in a bottle.*

She had gone to see one of those slasher movies with Phil early on when first dating. Phil had liked the idea because he thought it would end with her jumping into his arms, not knowing how scared she would be. Instead, any time he tried to reach across her leg to hold her hand, she almost jumped over the seat in front of her. It hadn't been as romantic as he'd imagined.

Later they had laughed about it, he swore he was not trying to scare her, just hold her hand, but she'd always wondered if he had been trying to scare her. It was the one thing about him that she mistrusted after all these years.

Facing the door, she screamed. Very loud, and whatever it was in front of her darted to the left. It had been behind her the entire time, a shadow covering the entire door. She could not understand what it was, but it was darkness, and she was most definitely afraid of the dark.

Backing up, no longer thinking about the exit, she tripped over the stand beside the basement door. She saw one shadow slink under the couch, then another. She was trapped and she knew it. She chanced screaming again as she ran for the kitchen. Her plan was to just run and head out the back door.

Phil heard the first scream, and a second one that was cut off midway when Mary's hand hit the basement door and closed it partially. The feeling of pain in her hand had caused her to stop screaming.

She would never know that if she'd just kept screaming,

she'd have had a chance. The shadows may not have continued to chase and consume her.

Seeing the door in front of her, she had time to think *I'm gonna make it* before she saw them following after her. Yanking it open, she ran outside, took a quick breath, and headed for the car. Getting the keys out, she pushed the remote start button.

Never once did Phil enter her mind. She was on pure instinct then. She was being chased by the dark, and she would not let it get her. *There are monsters in the dark* she thought.

The headlights of her car seemed to keep the creatures out of her direct path. She sensed them more than saw them beside her and around her. Running faster than she thought possible, she reached the car in record time, pulling open the drivers' door, jumping in, and throwing it in reverse. She cut the wheel as far as she could, trying to do the turn she'd seen often on the cop shows they watched a lot. The car almost stalled out as she got it in drive and headed down the driveway.

Mary turned on the dome light then, shaking as she was driving faster and faster away from the house. She was about a mile down the road, not sure where she was headed, when she called Phil's cell phone.

In the darkness, Phil's pocket lit up by the ringing of the phone he would never answer. His hair was grey, his face wrinkled almost beyond recognition, as the shadow consumed him.

"Come on, Phil," she yelled, hanging up, and dialing 911 next. Mary was a good driver. Almost a great driver. Her dad wanted her to drive in some of the dirt track races but she had lost interest after turning thirteen. But she hadn't forgotten what he'd taught her. Watching the road, high beams on, she flew around the turns. She was not sure where she was going, but she was driving well.

"Nine one one emergency. How may I help you?" the operator asked.

"Something's in my house, at One twenty two Whitacre

please help," she said, letting out a sigh she didn't know she'd been holding.

"Yes, Ma'am, sounds like you are in your car. Where are you now? We will send someone."

Seeing a sign ahead that she could not quite make out because of the dome light, she held her hand up to block its glare for a second. Just one second, and that was all the creature needed. It had been making its way in through the engine compartment, into the ventilation system.

The creature followed the shadow cast by her hand on the dash into the car, down her arm, numbing it and devouring her before she could let out a scream.

Later, the police would say she must have been drinking, due to the bottle of bourbon found at the crash. It had been empty; but that it had been Phil's empty. The police had had no way of knowing.

"Must have been doing one-twenty," the officer said to his supervisor. Straight into a tree, didn't even try to turn.

"The movie was good," she texted her Mom. "Going to eat, staying at Lucky's. Did you talk to Dad about Roy yet?"

CHAPTER 6
SLEEPOVER

Lucky smiled. She was having such a great night. Top down, hair blowing. Ginger sat in the passenger seat beside her, and Kane sat in the middle on the backseat.

"Home?" Kane asked.

Both Ginger and Lucky looked at each other and in unison said, "Nope!" Ginger finished with "Gonna be a long day on the farm for you tomorrow, Kane. You are ours!"

In the mirror, Lucky mouthed "Sorry," and laughing, headed out toward Johnson's Lake. Her dad had a small cabin there. She had texted her mom earlier, letting her know she would be at Ginger's. It seemed silly to lie since she was in college, but no need to let her dad know that she would be staying in the cabin with "a BOY!"

She handed her phone to Ginger, who typed "Love you, goodnight," before sending another text to her mom saying the same. Ginger did not notice that the previous message had not been read.

"Get ready to go into the dead zone," Lucky said, and Ginger started counting bars on her cell. "Four strong, three," laughing she said "holding at three. Did they add another tower?" she asked just before she added "Nope, zero bars."

"I see why your dad likes this cabin, Janet," Kane yelled from the back over the road noise.

"Who's Janet?" Ginger asked and continued, "I mean, come on Lucky. I think that Kane's lost it. Talking to this Janet again. If I were you, I'd get his head examined."

Lucky had prepared earlier in the day. Her plan originally had been just for her and Kane, but with Roy being so creepy, she did not want to take Ginger home, so the plans had been altered a bit. When they got to the cabin, she took charge. "Kane, take the gas can off the side of the jeep and get the generator going. I'm sure Daddy has some, but I don't want to run him dry," she said and then to Ginger, "Give me a hand with the cooler. I've got some beer and other food."

"Will there be bacon?" Kane asked. "I love me some bacon!"

"There is always bacon. Get to work," she finished.

Within a few minutes, the generator was on, lights were on inside, and the fireplace was lit.

A pile of blankets on the floor in front of them as they sat in a semicircle, talking. Lucky, who was in the middle, leaned against Kane, his arm around her waist, trying to be low-key about it. He didn't want Ginger to feel bad that he and Lucky were closer.

Lucky's wrist was hurting again. A dull ache she just couldn't shake. That feeling something was going to go wrong. *Must be because I'm so happy right now. Stop waiting for the other shoe*, she admonished herself.

"Tell me about the parties! And the boys," Ginger demanded, startling Lucky out of her thoughts. She had gone away for a second. Looking behind her, she swore that someone was watching her, but that was impossible with the windows boarded up. Her father did that for winter and he had not been up yet that year.

"Well, there is one Dad wants to kill," she said, rubbing her wrist before telling a modified version of the party and how she had flipped Jerry in the parking lot. She made it seem like she had not been looking forward to seeing him that night and that it was a misunderstanding. "More funny than bad," she finished.

Looking around again, she said "Fudge, I forgot my backpack in the jeep. I'll need my flashlight later when visiting the outhouse, excuse me, the ladies' room." Smiling she started to stand, but was slower than Ginger, who popped up.

"I've got it, you both need some alone time and I need to, well you know," she finished.

As Ginger headed toward the door, Lucky almost said, "Stop. Don't go!" but Kane picked that moment as he pulled her to him for their first real kiss. It was amazing and wonderful and all the things that she had hoped it would be.

"I love you Janet Lucky Evans," he said with such force that it nearly drove her back. It wasn't the volume, but how vehemently he said it.

Not knowing what to do or say, and ever being one to joke when nervous, she asked, "Who's Janet?" and they both laughed.

Feelings are there! Check! Yes! He loves me! I knew it! I'm gonna be a farmer's wife! No, I'm going to be a great farmer's wife who is also a… gotta pick a college major, fudge. She thought, all her thoughts running together as he took her face in his hands and kissed her again. This left a blissful silence in her head.

Outside, Ginger took her time. "Not much of a ladies' room," she said to the night, headed toward the jeep while she looked around. She had not inherited her mom's fear of the dark but was respectful of it.

Nothing was there. Reaching the jeep, she noticed Lucky's cell phone on the console. She had forgotten to hand it back. She grabbed it and saw a text. Using their common phone code, she unlocked the phone and thought *it must have come through when we topped that rise, and of course, no one heard it.*

As she read the text, Ginger began to get a strange feeling. She never got the feelings Lucky did, but the simple text read. "Come home now. Please drive safe, but come home and bring

Ginger." It was the portion indicating to bring Ginger that freaked her out.

Why mention me? If it was an emergency, a family emergency, they would just say come home, or call us even, but the come home now and bring Ginger. Her migraine came back, worse than last time. She was going to have to tell her mom. Not that she would believe her.

Ginger turned toward the cabin and could not believe what she was seeing. There was a dark cloud going around the cabin. Just circling, going across the roof, down the gutters, under the porch, behind the shutters, and around and around. The cloud made such wonderful patterns in how it circled the house.

She lifted Lucky's phone, wanting to capture the beauty of the dark cloud. She had heard of odd things in this world. Ball lightning, small twisters that had been known to pick up things, one had picked up her cousin's doghouse with the dog and all. It had carried them about sixty feet and set them down. "No worse for it," her cousin had said.

She turned on the video for the phone and started recording it going around and around. It was so beautiful, so majestic. *There are two of them, Lovers* she thought. *No, children playing,* noticing how they kept wrapping together.

Strange for clouds are they something else? she wondered. She could feel their desire to get inside, but something was keeping them out. *What is it?* she thought and then out loud said, "The light?"

With that, the shadows noticed her. She kept recording as they moved to circle the jeep and her. Stepping forward towards them, she whispered, "Beautiful."

As they started to circle her more closely, she dropped the cell on the ground without even realizing she'd done it, and she held her hands out wide. They encircled her hands, running through her fingers, and through her hair. Going between her legs and then up and around her head.

She giggled as one of them touched her on the back of the neck. Causing a grey streak to appear in her hair. She did not notice this because of the warm feeling it gave her. "Such euphoria," she whispered again and, "Thank you," as she noticed, her migraine was gone at last. A wonderful feeling of contentment washed over her.

Inside, Lucky and Kane were kissing, and with his strong hands around her, she knew if she did not stop this soon, she wouldn't be able to stop herself.

Pulling back, she asked, "Where's Ginger?"

Kane took a second to understand her words, then another to compose himself. "Sorry, ma'am. Didn't mean to muss you up. I'll go check."

Standing up, they walked towards the door, as Lucky's mind started screaming for him not to open it.

When he did, she saw the shadows, the absence of light circling Ginger, going around and around as it slithered up between her legs, then around her back. They watched as her hair turned completely white, as the creatures coiled around her. Every time they touched her, Lucky swore she saw another wrinkle on Ginger's face, her hands. *She's aging,* Lucky thought, stunned in the doorway.

Kane was a man of action, having grown up a logical farm boy and trained to be a provider, and he was not frozen at all. He took in the situation, thinking *Whatever they are, they are bad, dangerously bad, and hurting Ginger.* Pushing Lucky back inside, he bolted outside and, making very little noise, grabbed Ginger by the waist. He thought to quickly grab her, thought she must be in pain, must be wanting their help but unable to scream. He just wanted to pull her back in the cabin.

Ginger, noticing the door open, smiles when she saw them. Trying to speak *"Aren't they amazing?"* but her mind unable to grasp that she was frozen by she shadows touch.

Kane grabbed her by the waist. The connection was broken, the pain she felt and the loss she felt was terrible "NOOOOOO!"

she screamed and started to punch him on the back and shoulders as he carried her toward the cabin.

She fought him, her snow-like hair flying in all directions as she clawed at his face with her long nails *How did they get this long*? she wondered.

Inside, he tossed her toward the couch. Wanting to get rid of the wildcat he'd picked up, he turned and slammed the door.

Looking around, *Where's Janet?* he thought.

Lucky had snuck outside; she needed to see better and had realized that part of the problem with seeing them was the light. When Kane picked up Ginger, Lucky jumped off the porch and headed towards the tree line. She wished that she could have told Kane the plan, but whatever was going on, she knew this was what had been after her before.

Once in the woods, she turned back toward the cabin, and they were slithering on the ground where Ginger had been, *looking for the scent*, she thought. They must have found it because they started to circle the cabin.

They slinked over the roof, slithered around the shutters and, like some type of worm, got under the porch. She was unsure why they didn't enter the cabin, there were a lot of openings, and then she realized it was the light.

Great I am in the dark, and those things are afraid of the light, she thought, as she scolded herself.

Inside, she heard Ginger scream, such a longing scream, like she'd lost a lover and was wailing for him to return.

Kane had rescued Ginger just in time. Her hair was snow white, and she had a lot of wrinkles on her face. If Kane had not known better, he would have said she was in her forties, someone prematurely grey.

"They love me. They are so beautiful. Let me go, Kane. Please, I beg you, my children," she pleaded.

She's lost it, Kane thought.

When he did not get out of the way, she turned back toward

the fireplace, grabbed the poker, and cried, "I'll kill you," she spat and charged him.

They circled around and around each other. Kane did his best to not hurt his friend. *What the heck is going on?* he thought and *where is Janet?*

Lucky was outside, moving silently toward the jeep. Her father did not want a boy, but he refused to let anyone grow up on a farm that did not know how to hunt and provide for themselves. Moving silently came naturally to her. It was almost as if her body knew where not to step. Which branch to avoid because it would snap. She used every bit of her skills and finally reached the jeep.

The top was down, the jeep between her and the cabin. She reached in and grabbed the flashlight out of her backpack. *One hundred and twenty thousand lumens, Let's see how you like this* she thought, not daring to say anything aloud.

Inside, Kane had his hands full, he did not want to, but he thought he was going to have to hit Ginger to get her to stop. He steadied himself, ready to take a blow to his arm and sacrifice it, for the first time in his life, he was terrified.

Ginger was not looking at Kane, she was looking at the light beside her, smiling, then giggling. Something had clicked in her brain and she knew that the lights were keeping them out. Kane reached for the fireplace poker too late.

Lucky was just about to turn on the flashlight to find out if one could kill a shadow with a super bright light and sputtered, "Oh shit," aloud as the lights in the cabin went dark.

She heard Ginger's laugh, more of a cackle, as the creatures seemed to ooze through the walls into the cabin.

A second passed before she was able to move. The feeling of loss hits her, and she had a feeling that they were dead, but then the door shatters outward as Kane bursts through it. He carried Ginger and ran toward the jeep. "Start her up!" he shouted. The creatures were on his heels, toying with him. She pictured two cats playing with a mouse and screamed "THAT IS MY MAN!" while turning on the flashlight.

Everything was covered in light. Kane, almost tripping in the sudden bright light, he managed to move to the side, as both creatures were frozen in place. The light covered a wide area, and there was nowhere for them to go. Lucky studied them in the light and, after a few moments, noticed them getting smaller as the light hit them dead on, stopped them and eventually burned through.

Just like the smudge on my arm she thought but did not take time to look. She was busy holding the light on them. Kane went around her and got in the jeep. Taking out his pocketknife, he cut one of the back seat belts and tied Ginger's hands to the roll bars.

Ginger stared at the creatures; as she watched them, she knew they would soon be dead. "My beautiful, wonderful shadows!" she screamed at Lucky.

"Stop, Lucky, please stop, come on, Lucky. STOP! Please stop," she pleaded, then screamed louder. "My babies. Don't kill them. Please don't kill my babies!"

At the last bit, Lucky almost stopped; there was such pain in Ginger's voice. Ginger, understood that Lucky would never stop, said in a flat, toneless, voice that sent chills down Lucky's spine, "I'm going to kill everything you love, Janet. Do you understand me? I'm going to kill everything you love, and then I'm going to kill you!"

Keeping the light on the creatures, Lucky started to cry. She did not know what was going on, but she knew was that she had lost her best friend and things would never be the same.

Lucky moved forward, she wanted as much light on the shadows as possible, as she watched them finally die. Nothing left. Turning back to the jeep with tears streaming down her face, she saw that Ginger had passed out.

Kane was in the driver's seat, jeep started. "Let's go," he said, calmer than she could fathom.

Just then, across town at Ginger's house, Officer Conrad walked up to the front porch and into his mic reported, "Dispatch Twenty-One I'm ten dash six at One twenty two Whitacre to notify the family and while multiple vehicles are around no answer. Power is off, going in to investigate."

"Ten dash four Officer Twenty-One," the mic squawked back.

Inside the residence, Officer Conrad pulled his sidearm. Something was not right. He felt it in his bones, as people often said. He panned his flashlight around the room.

As the primal fear hit him, he felt it coming up the stairs. *A lion,* he thought. *Someone let a lion loose in the house,* he placed his feet in a shooter's stance, held the Glock up, finger off the trigger but ready to fire, as he waited.

He saw the shadow of the animal. *That must be it,* he thought, and it took him a second to register that the animal was the shadow, and it felt just like that time his brother had picked up that bear cub.

His brother had been holding and petting a baby bear cub in the field. He had never been able to spend much time in the woods after that. He was too nervous and never wanted to see anything like the power of the mama bear standing in front of them.

He, at fourteen, knew better when his brother, nine, had not. "Don't move," he'd whispered, "Don't move and let it go."

The bear had seemed much larger than it was, he was sure of that, but back then, it had felt ten, maybe fifteen, feet tall and all teeth. After becoming an officer, Conrad had fought gang members, dove into the middle of fights, been shot twice, and had been doing whatever he needed to do to maintain order his entire career; he was a tough guy. Everyone knew it.

Into his mic he whispered in a quivering voice "ten dash one," and closed his eyes. Praying for the first time since the bear. Ten dash one is the code in his district for help "Officer needs assistance."

Later he would swear that he'd seen something, but it was

moving too fast to make out. Describe an animal, small bear, large dog. He'd later lie and say the door was open, but he knew the truth.

It was darkness straight from hell on its way to pull someone back into the seventh circle of hell.

It was the darkness, but it also felt like it was the mama bear, on its way to protect her cub and God help anyone in the way.

The following Sunday, Officer Conrad picked up his mother and took her to church for the first time in years. During the service, he began to openly weep, and turned towards his mom to hug her as he laid his head against her shoulder, not bothering to hold back the tears. He was thankful the darkness had not wanted him.

On the way back home, Lucky reached for her phone on the dash, and it is not there. "Do you have your phone?" she asked Kane.

He shook his head no and said, "Left it in the cabin, I don't think we should go back for it. Just in case."

Lucky said, "Stop the jeep," and picked up the flashlight, she begins to undress. "Lucky now is not the time," Kane said nervously.

"Oh stop," she scolded him, then added, "Shine the light on me, look for any shadows or smudges." There was one on her wrist. She knew it. It must have happened at Ginger's house. They got out of the jeep, and she had Kane pull off his shirt, exposing his muscles and shined the light on him. He also had one on the arm that he had put around Ginger's waist.

Kane was amazed as he watched it disappear in the light. "What is going on?" he asked.

"I don't know," Lucky responded, as she stepped into the jeep. Her top was off, but her bra was still on. She looked at Ginger, who was covered in the smudges. "Quickly help me," she shouted to Kane, as she sensed something on the way.

She undressed Ginger, who was passed out, they shone the

light over her. Lucky finally relaxed as the last smudge disappeared.

She hugged Kane and finally felt safe. Neither of them noticed Ginger as she stood up, the pocketknife was in her hand. She found it in Kane's shirt after he'd taken it off and dropped it on the ground. Not thinking, they had laid her on top of it while undressing her.

She stepped toward and stabbed Kane twice in the back, laughing. She turned and said in that calm voice, "Everyone and everything you love," before running into the woods.

In the room, surrounded by light, the witness said, "Everyone and everything she loves, everyone she loves, everyone you love." At the same time, he scratched his arms and began to laugh.

CHAPTER 7
THE CHOICES WE MAKE

Kane kneeled on one knee, and their shirts mingled with Ginger's clothes on the ground at his feet. He looked up at Lucky. "I'm sorry. Didn't think she would go this crazy," he said.

Lucky, bent down, grabbed her shirt from the ground, and pressed it against his back. "Hold on," she said, as she started to cry. "Hold this," she placed her hand on his back. She ran to the jeep, saw the uncut seatbelt in the back, and quickly sliced it clear. She used both their shirts, along with the seatbelt, to get the bleeding to stop before helping him up and into the passenger seat.

He groaned as she laid back the seat a little. "You want to keep pressure on it, hon. Stay with me," she said while she tried to hold back more tears.

Starting the jeep and pulled out on the road, shouting over the gravel noise said, "Let's get you to the hospital!"

"NO!" he said more forcefully than she thought possible in his condition. "Home! She may head there. Get us to your house now!"

She knew he was correct, knew that her parents were in danger, but she still thought to herself, *please don't make me make this choice. Not now, after we finally found each other. I don't want Kane to die.* She started to turn left at the intersection that would have taken them to the hospital. She knew the correct choice as he touched her hand on the gear shift.

She turned right and pressed the gas pedal all the way down, going through the gears quickly, getting up to speed. "You know if we keep cutting seatbelts out of this jeep, it won't be safe to drive," he joked and coughed as he wiped blood from his mouth, and he tried to cover it up so she would not see.

They were almost to her home when she noticed Kane, almost asleep in the passenger's seat "Stay with me," she said. "We are close now."

Popping over the hill, she expected to see the farm mostly in darkness, illuminated only by the few pole lights meant to keep people from stealing a tractor or animal or both. But she was surprised to find the place was completely lit up, and several cars were in the driveway.

She saw a couple cop cars, some dogs, along with her Uncle Ed's Mustang convertible, which was covered in rust, but had once been a beautiful car. Lucky always hoped to restore it with him.

Lucky wondered how they knew what was going on. She could see the visible relief on her father and uncle's faces when she pulled up. Her mom would be inside getting ready to feed an army.

She slammed on the brakes of the jeep, pulling it to a stop, then got out, barking orders. "He's been stabbed, Ed; get your kit. Dad, help me get him into the house!" but no one moved.

She was about to say something to get them moving when her mom yelled. "You heard her; I'll clear off the table. Lucky for goodness's sake put a shirt on."

Lucky looked down and discovered she was standing with all the important men in her life, along with a lot of men and boys she did not recognize, wearing only her bra. She had chosen an adorable one at least, not knowing how far things might go with Kane earlier that night, which seemed like a long time ago to her.

She turned around, headed for the passenger door, her face was beet red, she heard her father close behind her say, "You have some explaining to do darlin', but right now let's take care of this boy. You know I may have to kill him later, and I want him well for that." He took his jacked off and wrapped it around her.

Later, she will think about that moment, inhaling his scent, knowing how much he loved her.

"Yes, Daddy, please save him so you can kill him." Tears started down her cheeks again. She opened the door, and her father reached in, unbuckled the seatbelt, and picked up Kane before turning around and heading toward the kitchen.

Lucky could not believe her father's strength as she watched her father carry Kane up the steps and into the house. Kane was a big man, but her father looked like a groom carrying a bride across the threshold right then.

Outside, she heard Sheriff Madagan talking into his radio. "Two found, still two missing, dispatch." She missed the rest of the conversation as Uncle Ed came through the door and closed it.

He had been a medic in the service. He'd told her that if he was going to train to be able to kill, he wanted to make sure to be able to save.

"What happened?" he asked, and Lucky told him. Not who stabbed Kane, or anything that happened before, but that he was stabbed, and to her, it appeared as if they went straight in and out of two different spots. With that done, Ed and her mom took over.

Lucky's father was a lot of things, but a medic he was not. Turning, he walked Lucky over to the sink, held her hands under the water, and started cleaning the blood off them. Then he used a dish towel to wash the blood and tears from her face.

"We only have a few minutes before the sheriff comes in. Tell me everything, and I'll catch you up on what everyone was doing here," he said to her in a voice so calm he could have been explaining how to boil an egg.

"You won't believe me," she started, and her dad frowned before he turned the water all the way hot, pushing her hand under it. She pulled back as it burned her, and he continued in that calm voice.

"I know two things, Lucky. That water is hot, and you don't lie when it counts. So, spill it. We don't have time."

Lucky told him everything, leaving out nothing, even the kiss. She did not notice Uncle Ed's hands shake when she talked about Ginger crying over the loss of her babies. He never talked about his time in the military. Ed only spoke of it as in—I learned this in the service or, because of the service I know how to do that. He never told stories of what he had done. She didn't know whether he spent all his time on base or if he was in the thick of it.

She did know that he had bad nightmares, and her father was afraid for him. Not scared of him but scared he would forget where he was and hurt someone.

"I'm only scared of one man on this planet, Lucky, and I'm glad that mom told him he was not allowed to beat me up," her father had joked with her over the years, and Lucky knew there was truth in that. He wasn't afraid of being hurt; he feared Ed losing control.

Lucky finished the story with her father's arms around her, holding her as Ed and Kate continued to work on Kane.

Her father told her how Ginger's mom had been in an accident, burned beyond recognition. He told her about how they'd found out that before the accident, she was on the phone with dispatch talking about something being in her house.

He talked about how Officer Conrad described some type of black bear running out of the house. "You remember him? He won the shooting match," he started to say when interrupted by Ed.

"Cheated! I thought it was just traditional sights. If I'd known we were allowed all that fancy modern crap I'd have won," Ed said. Lucky could see him stitching up Kane's back now. Everything was cleaned out.

"Ed, that was a long time ago. That was not my point. Just letting Lucky know the context for my next statement. I heard him on the scanner, Lucky. He was scared; I've never heard that man be afraid, and if it had been a bear, he'd just have shot it. Either with a pistol or a shotgun. Best shot I know."

There was a cough at the table and Lucky knew it was not Kane or her mother, as her father finished, "Okay, second best shot." Ed was smiled.

Lucky's mom had been quiet most of the time, just helping. She would have made a fine nurse; they all knew from experiences living on the farm. Over the years she had helped Ed fix the cuts, bumps, and other things. She finally spoke. "You said she appeared to age, right?" she asked and continued when Lucky nodded yes, "I think I know why Ginger went off like she did."

Everyone stopped moving to listen intently. "Do you remember when Roy's fingers were broken, Lucky?" she asked, and Lucky did. He had to wear a cast for a while and milked it whenever she was there, wanting her to help him get dressed. Even at an early age he was a creep.

She told her she did, and Kate continued, "All of you except Joe heard he was running through the house and tripped, jamming his fingers in the door. The reality was he had been running through the house and his mother, having had enough of it, shoved his fingers in the door and slammed it. It could have been a lot worse, and she did not tell anyone what she had done until a couple weeks later, when she told me. She told me because she was afraid of what she might do next. Remember, from then on, I never let you stay there. You and Ginger came here. I got her an appointment at the doctor's office, and a couple weeks later she had surgery. She had some type of tumor.

The thing she said that stuck with me all these years is 'how beautiful his little fingers sounded snapping in the door frame.'"

Lucky could not believe what she was hearing. Ginger's mom was the nicest person she knew. Her mom continued on, finishing the story with, "She said her mom had been the same way. That one day she just snapped. Back then, people didn't go in for X-rays, they took different mommy helper medication. Her mom, Ginger's grandmother was—"

"Mean as a snake," Ed finished for her.

Lucky's mind was racing again. So, Ginger could be saved. The poor thing had lost it all and did not even know it yet. She had to find her and get her the help she needed.

Just before Sheriff Madigan opened the door, Lucky's dad told her, "They were looking for the two kids and came here. We had gathered everyone to coordinate a search."

"What have we got here Ed? He gonna make it?" Sheriff Madagan asked as he came into the room.

"Yes, he won't be able to have sex again, but that has more to do with Joe, than with his current injuries," Ed said flatly, winking at Lucky, who turned red again, as she headed to her room to change.

"I'll want to talk to you, miss," he started when Joe stepped in front of the sheriff and demanded, "Where are we with the team?"

The sheriff knew that trying to get past Joe would be like beating his head against a wall, so he began describing what they had found so far in the house. "No sign of the boy, and now that we know the girl was at the cabin, we can start our search there. Who stabbed Kane?"

"Ginger did. I think something else is going on here, Sheriff. I'm not sure what. Maybe it's something in the water over there or in the air? Gas leak?" Joe said.

"PCP," Ed shouted. "I bet that boy. What's his name, Roy, got some when he was in New York and dosed his family. I've seen what that can do. You know, military experiments."

Joe looked at his brother and wondered if some of this was a part of the things he did not discuss. He had heard about all kinds of experiments in the 60s and earlier, but not in the modern age.

"Okay," Sheriff Madigan said nervously, he had always been leery of Ed, and this was just another example of not knowing if he was as crazy as he put on, as dangerous as they said, or just all bluster and bullshit.

There was a story about when Joe was young. Both had gone to one of those topless joints across the state line. Joe would be married soon, and Ed was about to enter the service.

Both had had more to drink than they should have before a bunch of football players from the Hornets had come in. All would have been well, but one of the boys got handsy with a girl that Ed fancied.

"Ed, let it go," Joe told his brother when he squared off against the player. "Let's get out of here," he said, getting in between Ed and the center.

Sammy J, the center, was supposed to go pro the next year. Joe had recognized him, and had rooted for the team over the years. They were local heroes. *Not really bad boys*, he thought.

Turning back to face Sammy J, Joe would have apologized and offered to buy them a beer. He did not want to get married with a black eye or worse.

Sammy J hit Joe on top of the head with the beer bottle he had been holding instead. Joe was a big man, but it caught him right, and he was out. He'd hit the ground like a sack of potatoes.

Seeing this, Ed smiled and said, "Now you've gone and done it. He was the only one keeping you out of the hospital."

There were seven of them. Five went to the hospital. The only reason the others did not go is they ran at the start of the fight when they saw Ed's viciousness. The center would walk with a limp for the rest of his life, and his jaw would hurt if he didn't cut his steak very thin.

The owner of the bar said after. "He did it with his bare hands. They picked up bottles and chairs, and one had a knife. I think that if it had not been for the knife, they would have arrested him, but since he was headed to boot camp the next week, they let him go. Best he kills for our country, ya know. He would have blinded Sammy if I hadn't fired the shotgun in the air at the end. He had taken the others out. The ones that had not run already, and he turned back to Sammy, who was kneeling in front of him. The shotgun was only filled with rock salt, but it had made a loud noise and stopped him. He'd had Sammy J on the ground, thumbs in both his eye sockets squeezing. It was his smile, Sheriff, that got me. He was happy in the violence. Some men are I guess."

Shaking off the memory, Sheriff Madagan said again, "Okay," before heading out the door. Glad to be outside again, over his shoulder he yelled, "We will go look for the other two and talk to Lucky in the morning."

After Sheriff Madagan's exit, Ed and Joe carried Kane to the couch and laid him down, Kate covered him with blankets as Joe sat down in a rocking chair.

Ed sat on the fireplace hearth and said, "Well, that was fun. Joe sounds like what's coming next will be exciting. Are you gonna stay awake this time or let me have all the fun?"

Having finished covering Kane, Kate had been walking by on her way to sit on her husband's lap when she stopped and slapped Ed on top of his head. "I've still not forgiven you for that fight before the wedding," she said, and they all laugh, knowing it may be a while before they could relax again.

CHAPTER 8
PREPARING FOR THE ENEMY

ucky woke up stiff. She had been sitting on the floor in front of Kane while he slept. She'd been leaning back against the couch to hear him in case he needed something when she'd fallen asleep.

When she'd tried to move to one of the chairs in the night, he had placed his hand around her shoulder and neck to comfort either her or himself and, Lucky, not wanting to lose the connection, had remained.

It was still there when she woke as she glanced around the room. Her parents and Ed were in the kitchen, and the sunlight was starting to come through the window. Lights were on in the living room, and she guessed they would be on for a long time.

She did not want to move yet, it felt good with Kane's arm around her. She shut her eyes and leaned back a little.

In the kitchen she heard her uncle and dad talking. Every now and then Kate would interject something.

"Anything on the internet, Ed?" Kate asked.

Ed described a couple of sites in response, and what online encyclopedia said about them. How most of it was limited to folklore and that late-night show that he used to listen to on the radio when doing the long-haul driving. "I found a couple references to abductions, and spontaneous human combustion. Makes no sense those topics being related, but it's all I have so far."

"Looks like we are on our own," Joe said. "What do we know?"

"We know they can hear, or appear to hear, sounds. We know they stay away from light and hide in the shadows." Ed stopped speaking when Lucky came into the kitchen.

"And we know they can die. Light can kill them," she said with a smile.

"That's right, so we need a plan. The sun is just coming up, so we have the day. I assume the nights belong to the Shadows, and we'd best be someplace safe where we can control the light," Ed said.

"Don't forget there is another one. We have to be wary. Hopefully, she's not around, but who knows what she might try," Kate said before continuing calmly, "I spoke to Kane's mom last night. I did not go into it a lot but warned her as best I could. Even said it would be better if her and Grandpa headed up to her cousin's place for the next few days. Lied and told her that Joe and Kane would take care of all the chores on the farm."

"But, Mom, Kane can't," Lucky started, then realized that her mom already knew that but had chosen her words to ensure Kane's mother and grandpa got off to safety without having to worry about them.

Clapping his hands together twice, Ed says, "Okay, Joe, kids had the first round, what do you say? You gonna stay awake and fight with me this time?"

Kate raised her hand from across the room and said, "Ed, I will smack you again." They all smiled nervously and gathered closer around the table to discuss what to do.

A couple hours earlier, Ginger had been walking up to her porch from the woods. It had taken her a while to get there, and when she noticed the police, she'd decided to relax in the woods for a bit.

She felt another one of the beautiful Shadows someplace in the darkness, but it would not come to her, and she could not call louder.

After the last officer left, she came out of the woods and walked up to the porch, and instead of going inside, she turned and sat down on the rocker.

All the lights were off in the house. The generator had died several hours before and the officers had felt no reason to turn it on.

They had not found any bodies in the house, and it was assumed whatever Officer Conrad saw must have dragged them away. There had been some dust on the floor by some clothes that had not seemed relevant.

Sitting on the porch, Ginger started to sing quietly, calling to the creature, wherever it was. She sent out as much energy into the world as she could. Needing the Shadows to find her, to love her.

She knew that the two at the cabin were the babies, cubs if you will, and wondered if this was their mother, or their father.

Just as the sun was starting to rise, she saw it. Coming across the ground, wiggling under a car, under the tractor, *beautiful how it moved across the earth* she thought.

It reached the porch, and she stood, opened the door, and walked in, she turned toward it, and said, "Welcome to my home, won't you come in?"

The Shadow hesitated. It sensed no danger but took the time to assess whether or not it was a trap. Instinct told it that everything was safe; this one was different.

Ginger moved inside further and closed what was left of the door when the shadow entered. She moved to the basement and, without trying to turn on any lights, said, "Come on, I know where we can hide."

Standing, Ed said, "So that's it, I don't think we have a choice. Lucky, You and Kate stay here, keep an eye on Kane. If we are not back by sunset, stay with the generator on and every light you can gather. Guns as well in case you can't talk Ginger down or anyone else goes crazy." At this, Lucky winced. She did not want to hurt Ginger but knew she may not have a choice.

Ed continued, "Joe and I will go to the cabin and look for her first. If there were three of them, maybe the one at Ginger's headed to the cabin so we will try there first, and if we find it, we will kill it."

"If it's not," Joe took over, "we will go to Ginger's and check there. I'd like to just take a tractor and level the place, letting the sun get to every bit of it, but we still have to live here and deal with the sheriff."

"If it doesn't work, Lucky, you talk to Sheriff Madigan with Mom tell him you want Officer Conrad there. That you will tell everything if he's there. He may have trouble believing things, and you would feel better if an officer who saw something was there." Joe stopped to take a breath.

Ed finished with, "And whether he believes you or not. Do not let him take you out of this house. No matter what – you threaten to sue or whatever you have to do! Tomorrow morning, you take Kane, the tractors, and some dynamite and blow the F out of the cabin and her house. Push them down to the ground like they never existed. I'd bet my last dollar that it's in one of those, and can not picture it moving until it comes here. If my Mustang is not at the cabin, go to the house and do that one first. If we fail, the Mustang will let you know where we stopped. It has that gas kill switch I installed for my trip to New York, so remember, if you need it, you only have to flip it."

"If you are not here tonight, we will protect each other, and tomorrow, we will join Kane's family and figure out things," Kate promised solemnly, holding Joe's hand. Kissing it, she said, "I love you Big Wabbit."

Lucky looked confused for a second and then remembered their pet names for each other when they were in their teens. Picturing her parents young, she just wanted this to be over. It was not fair that she couldn't have that with Kane.

Ed and Joe reviewed everything they were taking before leaving in Ed's Mustang.

In a little plastic room, the witness laughed and said "The internet searches. That was how you all got into this, wasn't' it? I know when I came into the story. How could I have forgotten? I'm hungry again. Now, where was I?"

The man in white nodded his head to the staff, and they brought in his lunch or dinner, whatever it was. Difficult to keep track of time here. He looked at the trays they opened for the witness, which sickened him. He needed to hear the rest of the story, so swallowing hard, he said, "Go on, you can eat and talk."

Ed and Joe went to the cabin first; there was nothing there for them to find. Not even Lucky's cell. They assumed either Ginger, or one of the searchers had picked it up. They looked on the ground where Lucky said the shadows had died. They were both surprised that they could not see anything. The only hint of anything was the dog tracks. They were everywhere except for a six-foot circle in the dirt.

"See that?" Ed asked.

"Yeah, nice to know dogs can sense something. May come in handy," Joe said.

"Burn it?" Ed asked.

"Not yet," Joe said. "We stick to the plan; it'll be eleven soon and Ginger's house could take a while to search."

Shortly after, they arrived at the house. The lights were all off, but they had prepared for that. Ed set the generator on the ground and started placing lights all around. They left them off, with all the lights they had for Lucky's party, they should be able to light this place up.

"That gonna cover the roof?" Joe asked. "We don't know if these things fly or not. Lucky seemed to think that it was always attached to the ground or something but best to be safe."

"Yeah, I think it will cover everything. Now it won't help

with Ginger if she's here. We need to be prepared," Ed said as he kept working.

After he had everything set, Joe said, "Light it up!" and Ed turned on the generator, every light around the house set to shine on the walls, under the porch, and even in the open windows. "It may not help a lot during daylight, but it would be good at night. Remember, We need to refill it at six," Ed said, grabbing his flashlight and heading into the house.

The plan was that in every room they went into, they would yank down any curtains that were covering the windows. They both had multiple flashlights, some like lanterns, which would keep them covered in light as much as possible.

Ed, smiled and placed some fishing wire across the foot of the door before running it to a lamp on either side of the entrance. They had talked about this earlier. The generator outside was life, which would also be what Ginger would try to destroy if she were still alive. This would at least give them a heads-up.

Joe placed a similar trap at the back door and one at the foot of the steps. They had forgotten to tell Lucky this, but since their plan was to destroy the house, it should not matter.

Having taken down all the curtains on the ground floor, they moved upstairs. Thinking they would have a fifty-fifty shot, upstairs was the first choice.

Ginger heard them before she heard the generator kick on. She was not sure if it was the police or Lucky come back to finish her off. How could she have been such a good friend to someone as treacherous as Lucky? "What a bitch," she said quietly.

The Shadow stirs from its slumber. Ginger lays her hand on top of it and gently strokes its head and whispered "Rest easy big man, I've got this."

Seeming to understand, or maybe not being as active in the day, the Shadow obeyed and moved from on top of Ginger. She was weak when she stood up, but it felt so good. They would not find it in here she knew, but still, she did not want take a chance.

She left the subbasement. Her father and his before him were big into making moonshine. They did not think of it as illegal so much as it was their right to make and drink it; since the government did not like it, they would hide it.

Sanctimonious assholes, she thought. They would talk fondly about making booze and how her father had learned to drive running booze across the state line, hiding from cops in his seventy one Cuda, but let Roy have one small pot plant behind a shed and "How can you do this? That's against the law."

Yes, Ginger had known before that there were differences between them, but still. People sure were funny.

She shut the door to the subbasement quietly, putting the panel back in place. It had not been used in a while and if someone looked, they would be able to see the outline of a door, but at one time it had been completely hidden. *Good thing the lights are out.*

Deciding that her best bet option would be speed, she began to formulate her plan. If she could get outside quickly, destroy the generator, or burn it up, she would. Taking one of the fire starters off the fireplace mantel in the basement, she makes her way up the steps. The darkness prevented her from noticing that her long hair in the mirror was completely snow white. She felt her fingers, so much weaker than earlier, but assumed it was just because she did not get to sleep.

Finished upstairs, they see her, a banshee running through the door headed outside. Her left foot missed the fishing line, but the right caught it. She spun and drug the lamps to the ground. She rolled on the ground and started crawling toward the generator.

Once she saw the gas cans, she tried to free her feet just as Ed and Joe grabbed her. She screamed, and fought them. Like a wildcat, she punched, kicked and bit at them. Ed noticed a lot of missing teeth. "Fuck this is insane," he shouted to Joe, who was trying his best to contain her. Both had dropped their flashlights on the ground outside.

It was still a few hours until dark, but they could take no chances with her breaking the generator.

"I'll kill you, kill you," she screamed and snapped at the air. Ed finally got his arms wrapped around her. He was behind her and she kicked back at him, biting at Joe who was trying to tie her with the zip ties they had with them.

She let out a scream that pierced the night, then convulsed, cursed them, and died. Later a coroner would say a massive heart attack, strange for her being so young. No explanation for the long snow-white hair, or wrinkles. Just more things unexplained.

Ed lowered her to the ground gently, cursed aloud, and tried to catch his breath. "There wasn't anything else we could do, Joe. We tried."

"Now we know it's there, and it's in the basement. Been feeding on her all day, I guess. Think we should just get the tractors or head in? We have a few hours before dark. I've never been in their basement. What do you think?"

In the basement, the Shadow expanded, and filled the subbasement. It had fed well, and soon it would feed again.

If the creature had instincts and thoughts, its and Ed's were a perfect mirror-

Ed *trapped.*

The Shadow *trapped.*

"I'm not sure which thought the other was trapped," said the witness.

"Instinct or intellect?" the man in white asks. "It is important to know, keep going."

The witness laughed and laughed, the last one turned into a cackle, and reached a higher pitch than he would have thought he could.

The guards outside the plastic room all felt the same cold chill and nervously looked around for any possible Shadow. One guard was comforted by a small button with a sign on a chain. The sign had flipped over, and he wanted to turn it back to read it. But the superstitiousness of men in battle, and this was a battle of sorts, prevented him from flipping it and reading it. He knew it had been that way for an awfully long time. Not knowing exactly what would happen when the button was pressed, the guard was strangely comforted even if it meant his own death.

CHAPTER 9
TRAPPED

ucky dropped the glass she had just pulled out of the cupboard. It was just still a few hours before nightfall, and they were waiting for the sheriff to bring Officer Conrad over, when the glass just fell out of her hand, and shattered on the floor.

"Something's wrong," she said, and turned around to face her mom.

"Yes, you just broke one of our best glasses. It came in a set of eight and now we have four. Seems you and your father drop them, or he forgets his in the barn. I think one has paint thinner in it in the mop sink, so yes something is wrong," her mom joked.

"I mean it, Mom. You know I get these feelings. We need to go over there," Lucky pleaded with her.

Kate hugged her daughter, and then going to the closet, pulled the broom and a dustpan out. She started sweeping, thinking of what to say, when she heard a car in the driveway.

"Sheriff's here now, have to wait, Lucky," she says, trying to stay calm. "Stick to the plan, he has Officer Conrad with him, so tell him everything, and let's see what happens. Okay?"

Ed's hand ached. Forgot to take his meds this morning. He

shouted over the generator, "Getting old sucks. Joe, you ready?"

Joe stood up after putting the cap back on the generator. "That will hold us for about four hours. If it takes longer than that, I doubt we will need light," Joe said.

Both walked toward the porch with still a couple hours before nightfall. They had taken time to wrap the girl in a tarp and placed her over by the trees. Partly because they were not sure she would not come back, but also because she had been a good kid. They had wrapped her tight with some hay twine, and Joe had said a couple words over her while bowing his head.

"Seemed silly to do that for someone who tried to kill, but I hope someone says a few words over me," Ed said as he touched the first step.

Both had flashlights in each hand, lights tied around their necks, and a couple stuffed in their pockets. The ones in their hands were the brightest, but the others would do in a pinch, they hoped.

As he stepped through the threshold first, Ed never could have guessed that the pine floorboards would all collapse. He found himself falling into the basement. Joe reached for him, but missed, and almost fell in himself.

Later, if someone were to have investigated, they would have thought the boards in the house were hundreds of years older than they were. All the wood in the floor, including the braces, were paper thin, the top barely showing any age, but the underside was almost dust.

The nails and other metal rusted away to almost nothing. Ed did not notice any of this as he fell, his back hitting the side of the couch. If he had been a step or two left his head would have hit an end table, or he would have been impaled by a lamp. As it was, he was only stunned. The lights in his hands fell to the linoleum floor, one shattered and the other making the light dance, as odd patterns formed on the wall as it spun around before it stopped and faced the stairs.

Joe, looked down, and could not believe what had happened.

He started to run for the Mustang to get a rope to pull Ed up when he saw the creature. It was much larger than he expected, as it uncurled and reached out with a tentacle-like appendage toward Ed, who lay breathless on the couch.

Joe pointed his flashlight at the creature's outstretched arm, tongue, whatever it was, it recoiled as the light touched it.

Joe, kept it pointed it at the creature as it retreated into the basement further to avoid the light, yelled down, "Ed, you alive?"

Coughing, Ed said, "Yeah that took the breath out of me. Did you see the size of it? Should have just flattened the house."

"Well, let's do that next. For now we need to figure out how to get you out of there. Can you reach the light?" Joe asked.

Ed tried for it, but from under the couch he feels the creature strike. His arm went instantly numb. He jumped up, so that he was standing on the couch, and looked around, grabbed the light from around his neck and turned it on.

Joe had been covering him, but his hand and arm had cast a shadow onto the floor.

"How big is that thing, Ed? Or is there more than one?" Joe shouted.

Ed, turned his light on and grabbed another out of his pocket, shown them around the room. At first a wall appeared to be black, but the longer that the light touched it, the blackness oozes away, revealing the true wall. "The creature is covering the entire basement," he said flatly.

"Joe, you are not gonna like this, but you need to do exactly what I say. Understood, little brother?" Ed yelled without looking up, not wanting to take his eyes off the creature that appeared to be everywhere. It was in every nook and contour of the room. Wherever the light does not reach, the creature was there.

Ed continued, "Joe, you need to go and get the dozer now. You need to let the generators run. When I reach up, drop down one of your bright flashlights and then return to the Mustang.

Grab one of the lanterns and throw that down for me. With those, I should be able to start clearing a path to the stairs."

"Okay, but why not wait until you are up before I go? I can cover you from here," Joe said, he knew the answer but did not want to leave his brother.

"It's going to take me a long time, and we don't have time. If this thing gets out, or if you don't get back in time with the dozer, I feel this creature will win. You also need to tell Lucky and them what we know about its size and what it can do," Ed finished, reaching up as Joe dropped his flashlight onto his outstretched hand.

The creature tried to get to Ed in the quarter of a second that the light was falling, before Joe could shine his other. Still, luckily, it was not fast enough and had to slither back as Ed turned the light in that direction.

"Okay, get the lantern and head out," Ed yelled.

Ed covered himself as Joe dropped the lantern. It was already on and was very bright. Ed saw the walls behind him dissolve and turn into a soft peach color. The lantern looked like the old kerosene lamps but took batteries.

He held it in front of him and over his head a little, took the light from around his neck, and spun it behind him so that it was shining down on the floor. Then, using Joe's light, started to make his way off the couch.

The floor was concrete with linoleum flooring on top, so he guessed that the creature had not had time to age it into nothingness.

He could feel the creature everywhere that the light was not. Watching, waiting for him to make a mistake.

"Okay, Sheriff that's it. That is what happened exactly. Officer Conrad, could you have seen a shadow creature of some type and not a bear as everyone thinks?" Lucky asked, adding, "If it's like the others it's the size of that couch," and she pointed to the one that Kane was on. He was sitting up, and Kate was helping him eat.

Officer Conrad started to shake. He was trying not to lose his nerve and he put his hand on his pistol. For a minute there, Sheriff Madagan thought he was going to draw it. Thought he'd lost his mind, but then realized he was trying to work up the courage to say something. He had been Sheriff for a long time and knew people, and it worried him to see Conrad so nervous.

"It's as big as this room, maybe larger," Officer Conrad said quietly. Seeming to be afraid that talking about it might call it. Lucky's hands went to her mouth to stifle a scream; the sheriff's jaw dropped.

Kate looked up urgently, and said, "We have to go warn Joe and Ed NOW!"

"Lucky, you stay here with Kane. The rest of us will head over to Ginger's now. If it had been at the cabin and it has not killed them, they would have been back by now," she continued, frowning as Kane stood up.

"Kane you need—" she starts, and Lucky says, "Kane no," as she reached for him to help him sit back down.

Shirtless with just the bandages around him, Kane stood to his full height. The pain was unbearable but he did it anyway and in a voice well beyond his years, said, "Janet, get me one of your dad's shirts, and Kate, help me with my boots. We should never have divided."

"Sheriff, if you don't believe us and want to arrest us, can you do it tomorrow? We have a house to level and something to kill," Kane said.

Kane found his way to the kitchen and used the counter to lower himself into one of the chairs as Kate helped him with his boots.

Reviewing the situation, Sheriff Madagan decided he had no intention of arresting any of them, which was exactly what he tells Officer Conrad. At the same time, Janet and Kate continued to prepare. They laugh a little at Officer Conrad's confusion when he asked in all seriousness, "Who's Janet?"

Janet and her mom already had the tractor with a blade and a small dozer on the back of trailers ready to go. She had hooked them up, one to her jeep. It was a little small to pull it but since they were not going far, it would work. The other was hooked to her dad's truck.

Everyone rushed out of the house and loaded into the police car, truck, and jeep, except for Kate, who was still locking up the house. She had almost flipped the light switch off as she was shutting her kitchen door. She bit her lip, cursing under her breath. Just then, she heard the Mustang taking the turn into the driveway faster than she'd ever seen Ed drive it.

Flying into the driveway, Joe turned it around in time to see everyone loaded up. His wife jumped in the passenger seat. He opened the door and stood so that everyone in the vehicles could hear him. He described what happened to the floor and to Ed, and made it clear they needed to hurry. He cursed as he exclaimed, "Cell service is out it seems. I've tried to call to warn you to get ready. Should have known you would not wait," he said just before climbing back into the Mustang.

On the way there, he tells Kate that he wants her to keep going in the Mustang with Lucky, but Kate refused. "We are in this together, Joe. I should have been there today."

Joe frowns and she touched his hand lying on the gear shift. He's not going as fast as he wanted, holding back the rest could keep up. Kate added "I'm not mad, Joe, it's just that we are family and stronger when together. Ed is one tough sonofabitch, so don't count him out."

"Do you love me?" he asked.

"So much more than a bee sting," she said, kissing his hand. It was a little thing she used to say to him when first dating. He fell for her so hard and so fast and each day he had asked if she loved him more than a bee sting. Those days were long gone, but he smiled briefly at the memory.

Ed watched the creature spin, slither, and pulsate around him. He was not sure exactly how big it was, but even though the light hurt it, he did not know if dropping the house on it will do much. There had to be another hour until nightfall. "Come on, Joe," he said, reaching the stairs.

Not taking time to celebrate, he started to go up, remembered the collapsed floor, and stops. "The creature had this planned all along. Letting me get this far, knowing I would run up the stairs, and if they don't fall, the floor upstairs will. Like a fly to a spider, I guess," Ed finished aloud.

Ed stopped and knew the creature was not trying to kill him. That this was not about him at all. This had all been about Kane and Lucky. He was not sure how he knew this, but he just did. "Damn you! I won't be bait!" Ed yelled, as he tried to run up the stairs.

He kept his feet to the sides of the steps and hoped that they did not age as much while he tried to scale them, but they collapsed as he knew they would. He could have waited, but he knew that the amount of time they would have spent trying to save him would have let the sun set, and God help them if this creature gets out in the darkness after them.

It was Ed's only choice; it had been the same in that bar fight. He would have let those kids go as Joe suggested, but once they hit Joe and he wasn't sure whether he was alright or not, his decision had been made. You don't mess with family.

As Ed falls, the darkness that surrounds him is oddly comforting. He hoped his sacrifice gives them the time they need to kill it.

The Shadow's instincts took over as Ed fell, it wrapped around him, and absorbed him. Feeding off all that was Ed. Ed's heart is about to go, the light around his neck and in his hand doing nothing more than making the Shadow hungrier.

Ed laughed, and the creature stopped, sensing something wrong. Sensing that it should not have fed off this one so quickly. It starts to pull away, like a mouse, as it takes that first bite of cheese. The creature felt its end coming.

"You should just have let us go," Ed said, his hand shaking as he held the dynamite. He waited as long as he could, watching the fuse with eyes much older than he. "Shouldn't have messed with my family, Sammy J," Ed screams, his mind on the past as he threw the dynamite at the retreating creature.

The creature, trying to escape, felt the light and heat coming from the dynamite.

Ed never planned on this being a one-way trip, but he always tried to be prepared. Joe had a family, and they would look out for his little brother. So, he grabbed a few sticks while Joe said his goodbyes. Just two, and a lighter.

Such intense pain was not something the creature was used to. It had not hurt like this in longer than its mind could remember. This one. This one that he was using to catch the others had hurt him, he was dead, nothing more to feed on. The shadow howled a silent howl that only those like itself could hear the rage.

Joe heard the dynamite go off as he pulled to a stop, recognized instantly what must have happened. Holding his wife's hand, he silently prayed and stepped out of the car. Those few words for his brother, just in case.

Lucky heard the explosion, hoping what she feared was not true, and after stopping the jeep, the top still off, jumped out and ran toward the house.

Her father stopped her, explaining in a tone eerily calm considering the deadly situation, "He's dead, Lucky. It's gonna be dark soon. Don't let his sacrifice be for nothing."

Lucky recognizes this tone. This is the tone of the farmer. "The calf is dead; we have to save the mother. The south field has flooded; we need to save what we can." Lucky was familiar with that voice, being a farmer's kid and the worst for her over the years had been the funerals. She had hated her father when younger, not understanding him getting in crops after a funeral instead of spending time with the family, but later she understood. "For farmers, nothing stops. You have to keep going."

She looked at her father and, in the same voice, said flatly. "Kill it, Daddy."

CHAPTER 10
GRANDPA MILNER

Grandpa Milner sat in his room, watching the news. It seemed as he got older, he's started watching the news more, but he was unsure as to why. When he was younger, he would never have watched anything on the news, or picked a newspaper, he would rather be out on his bicycle with his best friend, but when older he just wanted to know what was happening in the world.

He ignored the ringing phone, figuring that it was not for him. Most of his friends were well past calling. He would go visit them this weekend if Ma wanted to. He did not remember when he started calling Kane's mom Ma, but it fit. It was some time after Kane's dad had passed. She had asked him to move in to help out. Kane being a great kid, did everything, so Grandpa really just got to retire. Every time he thought about it, he realized that was what her and Kane had really planned. They'd wanted him to stop working so hard and just live with them. He took to retirement better than he expected.

He heard her talking, excited at first. His ears were excellent. All of his senses were. He wouldn't let them know it, but he felt better than most people his age and, happily, did not have a suitcase full of meds that he had to carry. "Good Farm Living," he would say often.

Hearing her on the stairs, heading up to his room, he pressed the switch on the remote to go back to the channel that Kane had showed him. He would rather watch the news, but her reactions every time she entered the room were just too funny.

"Grandpa, we need to go too," she started and then "what are you watching? I'm going to put that on one of those news channels you used to watch and take the remote away!" she finished, exasperated with him.

She told him what little she knew. That Kane's been hurt, that they could not trust Ginger's aunt who looked a lot like Ginger, just older. She told him it would be best if they head out of town for a little bit since for some reason she seemed to be obsessed with Kane.

"Strange times," he said and, cutting off the TV, started to pack. "I'll be ready in twenty minutes. You should call Charlie and tell him to come by," he said.

"They said that Kane and Joe would take care of it..." she started, but Grandpa would not hear of it. "This farm has been in my family for longer than anyone can remember, and I'll be dammed if I let Joe Evans over here with his new technology. Who knows what he will do. He'd be liable to wire up the pigs. Call Charlie and tell him to plan for two weeks."

She looked at him funny, wondering if he knew more than she did on this, but with so much to do, she dropped it. They could talk on the drive.

Grandpa finished packing, took his suitcase down to the car. She told him she would be out in a few minutes and that she had already put her suitcase in the car.

He placed his suitcase in the trunk of the car, and climbed in the passenger side. Looking around, he rolled down the window with the hand crank, and closed the door. Leaning back, he relaxed. *It's still daylight, we have plenty of time* he thought.

The breeze was a little cool and it reminded him of another

time. A lifetime ago. *How had he gotten into that mess?* Grandpa Milner closed his eyes, remembering in a dream.

"Hurry up Henry Milner," Greg yelled as Henry ran for the train. Greg spotted the open door and without thinking, which was usually his style, said "Let's hop a train and blow this popsicle stand," he had picked up the reference from some TV show or movie that they had seen.

Greg, being leaner and overall faster, made it easily, jumping from his bike and running the last couple feet, diving, and just catching the door. He was yelling for Henry. Saying how he would go without him, and he would be a crappy best friend for letting him go alone on the train.

Henry got off the bike, but figuring they may need it, picked it up, placing it on his shoulder. He was a strong farm boy after all, so he may as well use those muscles. Then, running as fast as he could, he threw the bike and somehow Greg caught it.

Grinning, Henry almost tripped but recovered and having faith that his best friend would catch him, jumped for the door. Greg caught his left hand and pulled him in with the other. "You dork," Greg called at him, hitting him in the chest. "Why'd you bring your bike?" he asked.

Henry responded, "Well I like that bike, and Pa will tan my hide if I lose it."

Greg, sat down on the floor of the open train car, laughed and laughed and kept laughing until he finally spit out "You realize we are running away right? He will do more than tan your hide," and then both of them laughed until tears came to their eyes.

Henry had never planned on running away. Truth was his father was a fair man, and the farm was in his blood, but maybe just one summer adventure. After all he is almost grown, turning fourteen in the fall.

"Greg, this will stink if this just takes us into Marion and stops. Be a long ride back with you riding on the handlebars,"

Henry said while situating himself so that he could lean against the open-door frame and Greg on the other.

"I'm not sure where it goes, but this is day one of our grand adventure, and I would not go with anyone else." Greg said then caught himself being a little sappy and added, "you goober."

Henry laughed and told him that he needed to work on his material. The rhythm of the train felt nice, and, both being relaxed, they decided to shut the door to keep any riffraff out.

The train did not stop in Marion. Riding it through the day and into the night, both were hungry but decided to sleep and stick it out.

The next morning, they did not recognize anything when they opened the door, but it looked like they were headed east based on the sun. "Let's give it to noon. We will hop off and find some work. See where we are and work our way back home," Greg said, surprising Henry.

"Home?" Henry asked.

"Of course, we could jump on a ship and become sailors, but you know as well as I do that times are hard right, and farming is a good living. We will think of this as a vacation," Greg said.

It is clear to Henry that Greg was not into the grand adventure when his stomach was grumbling. He also knew that Greg was more sensitive than he was and was homesick already.

"When we stop and figure out where we are, you can call your mom and let her know we are okay. Just had been camping and forgot to let them know. Don't tell her where we are, but based on where we are you can say when we will be back. Then ask her to call my mom," Henry said.

He knew that it would make Greg feel better doing this, and he did not want to call his own mom or dad anyway. His ass was going to hurt, but taking off like this had felt good. Maybe when he turns sixteen, he may join the military. His uncle had lied and got in at seventeen.

Around lunchtime, Henry heard the whistle of the train and knew they did not want to be caught in the station, so both of them looked for as soft a spot as possible, threw the bike out, then jumped. They had both seen it done in many movies, so other than both almost breaking their necks they came out of it in fairly decent shape.

No one yelled from the train, so they had pulled it off, but where were they?

Henry, who usually had a good sense of direction, pointed, and said, "That way. March men!" like one of the drill sergeants from a movie they watched.

It did not take them long to find the road, and they quickly found out that riding on the handlebars at their size and age was not as easy as it was when kids. It was decided that one would ride and the other walk beside.

Crossing the top of a hill, they saw a welcome sign and after doing some quick math Henry said "You know we are a good three days walk from home. We may have to hitch a ride unless we can find a train back."

"Man, we are in so much trouble," Greg said, sounding even more depressed.

The road had a bunch of little hills and turns. Henry's mom would say that the person building the road must have followed a black snake.

Coming over the last hill, they saw a flattened-out area. Then tops of tents could be seen, and both exclaimed at the same time, "The Circus!"

"Well, you know you've always wanted to join," Henry said and they both laughed again as they headed into it.

"Are they shutting down or setting up?" Greg asked Henry when a very tall man walked up to them and said "We are setting it up for tomorrow, kids. You will have to come back then."

Seeing the look on their face when he said kids, he added, "I'm sorry, guys, but we will be here for a few days and then off to Marion for a couple, then off to another city. We don't stay anywhere long. Such is the life of circus folks."

Both Henry and Greg looked at each other and smiled. Henry took over, said they were both sixteen and working their way back home. Larry who it turned out was the Tall Man of the circus pointed them in the direction of the boss's trailer. They did not look sixteen to him, but as tall as he was, he could never judge age.

The next couple of days were a blur. Greg took to the circus life and told Henry when this was over he was going to join for real. They both enjoyed the hard work, the money would be good as well and that would help with explaining it to their parents both thought. The first night, after all the work was done, they made their way to town and called their parents. Henry figured that if they knew, they would have plenty of time to calm down and maybe not tan their hides as much.

No one liked the idea of them working at the circus on the way home, but Henry's dad thought it may be good for him. Especially seeing that other people worked hard as well so he could appreciate what he has.

What Henry would always remember was the different stories from everyone around the fire late at night. He knew that circus life was not for him, but he did enjoy the family aspect to it.

By the time they got to Marion, Greg had decided to stay. He told Henry that he was going to head back with him, take his licking from his dad, and then come back to the circus. He would buy his bike from him if they could not find his so that he could make it back faster before the circus pulled out.

Henry agreed, and after everything was done, sat down by the fire to listen to more of the stories for his last night. Looking around Larry smiled and said to Lavinia. "Please tell something scary. It is Henry's last night."

Both Henry and Greg listed intently to Lavinia. She was so mature and beautiful that neither could believe she was only eighteen. His mom would have said she had an old soul.

Lavinia, spit into the fire going into her fortune teller act. She told them that there is more to life than man understands. She talked of her parents fleeing their country. "We were down below Mexico when I first found the sight. My first experience with the spirit world was watching an angry spirit consume someone. I saw the man age a thousand years in the blink of an eye," she started, and Henry shivered, and felt like someone had stepped on his grave.

He was a good judge of people and whether someone was lying or spinning a tale, and even though what she said sounded impossible, he felt that it was real.

"The spirit came up from the ground of his ancestors. Just a shadow of what it once was and devoured him in front of me. The man was not strong, not brave, and not worthy so his ancestor devoured him."

When she said this, Henry got another chill. He knew that what she was about to say was important and that he would have to remember this. But the chill would not go away. So cold, he started to shake, looking into the fire, not feeling any warmth from it.

"Grandpa, put your window up or you will catch cold," Ma said, waking him from his memories.

Grandpa Milner could feel the wind from the window he had put down earlier. From surroundings he knew that they had been driving for a while.

"Have to remember" he mumbled to himself.

"Remember what?" Ma asked.

"Just the time I joined the circus, now when do we eat?" he said, trying to remember.

She did not ask but remembered the stories of how it had burned down. *We're due for a trip to the cemetery to visit his friends* she thought and placed her hand on his.

CHAPTER 11
HOUSE PARTY

Things happened quickly. Sheriff Madigan had Officer Conrad put flares out on the road and left the police car blocking the driveway with the emergency lights on. "No use having someone else drive in," he said getting out of his car. He grabbed a couple of flares and tucked them into his belt as he walked toward the house.

Kane, moved slowly, unloaded the tractor, while Joe and Kate unloaded the dozer.

Lucky, stood and looked down at Ginger's body wrapped in the tarp, tears streamed down her face. "Ginger and Uncle Ed no more, NO MORE!" she yelled. Filled with determination to kill the creature she headed toward the house. She knew it was still hiding there. Stopping at the Mustang, she opened the trunk, and sat the speakers on the ground. No one noticed what she was doing, they were all deep in their own thoughts.

The sheriff walked up to the front door carefully, peered down into the hole left by Ed, and shinned his light into the basement. He could see the creature swirling around, hungry with desire. "What are you?" he asked as Lucky turned on the stereo. The music blasted out loudly - something about needing a hero.

"What the—" he started and laughed nervously. He turned, and ran toward the Mustang yelling, "We have another weapon!"

He described to everyone what he learned. "I was toying with the Shadow. Just using the flashlight, and while it moved away from the light and appeared to be in pain, the light was not bright enough to stop it but when that music started, retreated into the back of the basement. This could help keep us safe and it contained after dark," he finished.

Joe smiling, said, "Then let's get to work."

Kane and Joe planted charges all around the house, while they kept a look out for little streaks of shadows. It was difficult because their own bodies were causing shadows so a lot of the time was spent shining their flashlights down to make sure that it was not the creature.

Kate and the sheriff kept an eye on the hole in the floor, comforted every time they saw it, knowing that when it is not there, they would have problems.

Lucky pulled the jeep to the other side of the house, opening the back, and exposed its speakers before she turned up her stereo. "All the way to eleven, bitches!" she screamed toward the house.

After placing the charges, Joe filled up the generator and looked around at everyone's solum faces "No need to let it run out. There is still a lot to do. We have some dynamite left for the end, but what we have set already will make a spectacular explosion. The rest we will save just in case we need it."

Sheriff Madagan turned to walk back to the lights, and Kate for an instant was in his shadow. Lucky screamed as she saw what is going to happen before it did, but she was too late. The darkness opened like a giant mouth from the doorway to swallowed her mom.

Joe turned toward Lucky's scream and, saw where she was looking, grabbed the box of leftover dynamite and ran toward the door. Determined that if he cannot save her, he would make sure this creature dies. *No one else dies today.*

Kate fell backwards into the pit before the sheriff could grab her. Joe knocked him out of the way, grabbed one of the sheriff's flares, before he leaped into the pit after his wife, case in hand. He saw her impaled on the lamp, aged beyond recognition. Knowing that she was dead, Joe says a silent prayer and turned toward the creature. If Sammy J had been there, he would have recognized the smile on his face as being that of his older brother.

The creature hesitated, perhaps out of fear, and the struck, and Joe could feel himself aging, could feel the pain in his ankles and his trick knee as it started to give out. *This is what it would have felt like every day had I grown old,* he thought as he pulled the flare, lighting it with the striker and then held it above the box of dynamite.

With his dying breath he shouted, "BLOW IT!"

Kane pulled Lucky back to the generator. It took all he could do to pull her behind the dozer. She wanted to leap in after to make the creature pay with her bare hands. Kane grabbed the detonator, then held it out to her.

She looked at it at first, not understanding what it was, and then with recognition said, "I love you." She knew that he could have flipped the switch, but it was better that it was her. It was fitting and meant more to her than any gift he could ever give her.

She turned off the safety, and pressed down the tiny plunger, and watched as the dynamite exploded around the house. Joe had tried his best to keep the blast in areas that would cause it to collapse in on itself. He had figured that if the inside was as weak as he suspected, that would work, and it did.

The walls came crashing down, and then in the basement the dynamite that Joe lit exploded. A cloud of dust rose up from the house and for a minute Lucky feared the creature may escape in it.

She ran for the dozer and Kane for the tractor, both moving as fast as they could to fill in any space left in the basement. Burying the creature and her family. She did not know if it would work, but sensed that the creature was like anything else. It needed space, it needed air, and it could die.

The Shadow was in pain, it felt ripped apart more so by the sounds of the explosions than by the fire. The fire hurts it as well, but it was the sound that has done the most damage. How could it survive? It felt the rumble of the dozer as they pushed the earth and house in upon itself.

It was a mere wisp of itself. No longer the leviathan it had been. These things have hurt it. *Have they killed me?* it wondered.

Maybe there was a chance. It could sense the darkness coming, it knew that before long it would be free to feed.

It moved and slithering through the small cracks, and debris in the basement as more and more of the house came down, it found the one that had first caused it real pain. How was this one still alive? The creature wondered. Still alive this one, just barely, and the creature needed to feed.

"Cut the engine, Janet," Kane yelled.

Lucky turned off the dozer, and smiled at him with her tear-stained, dust-covered face. It was a weak smile, but something.

She held onto him as they walked to the generator, checked its fuel level and put the tailgate down on her dad's truck. They both sat down, and she reached over to one side, opened her dad's cooler and pulled out two cans of beer.

"Got one more?" Sheriff Madagan asked and Lucky reached back for another.

"I think you got it," he said hopefully.

"We will not know until it's dark I guess," Lucky said and noticed for the first time it was well past dark. The lights that surrounded them and the house had let her forget the sunset. She was so tired. Holding Kane's hand, she knew that tomorrow or the next she would grieve, but she was a farmer's daughter, so she followed the ingrained edict: time to grieve when the work is done.

The sheriff took a long pull of the beer, drinking half the can before sitting, thinking, for a second. He took a look around, seemed to come to a conclusion, before saying, "We can't tell people what happened, they will put us in a padded cell and lock us all up if we do, so you both were never here."

Lucky looked up at him as he continued. "Kane decided to drive you back to college early. In fact, you should head there now. I'll call in a few days and let you know that there has been an accident. I will cover everything, so you do not have to worry. You and your family saved a lot of people, and the price was too high."

"But I—" Lucky began, when Kane, grabbing her hand, and held it in both of his, says, "Janet we have to go. He is right. If we stay and say anything this will turn into a shitshow. I'll take you back to college, stay with you until he calls us, and then we can figure things out. There is nothing else we can do here."

They waited with the sheriff for a few hours just in case it was not over. Sheriff Madigan had sent Officer Conrad with the gas cans for more fuel for the generator, and when he returned, the sheriff hugged them both, and said "Whatever you need, call me."

Lucky asked him to have someone take her jeep home for her. She told him to leave the music playing as loud and for as long as possible. If she was going to go, she would take Ed's Mustang.

Luck and Kane stood in front of the buried remains of the house holding hands. Their bodies casting long shadows in front of them while Lucky prayed for her parents and uncle.

Finally she turned grabbed her backpack and got in the Mustang. Leaning over, she kissed Kane and said, "We will go by and see your mom and grandpa before we head to the college. Let them know what happened. There is also something I need from my house." She pulled out of the driveway, and never looked back at what she had once considered her second home.

She knew that within a year the grass would be grown over the spot, and the raspberries that grew around the edges of the yard would be ready to pick.

Reaching the interstate, she noticed a couple of white SUVs going past. *Are those government trucks? But those are always black.* She dismissed them from her mind.

Officer Conrad passed the SUVs as well. He was on the way to the local fire station. The cell and landlines were all out and the radio was not picking up anything from dispatch. *Love to have me a white SUV someday* he thought as they went past.

Sheriff Madagan, sat on the tailgate of Joe's truck, third can of beer done, he saw them coming into the driveway. He knew that with the cell and landline service being out that there had to be more to this. "Ed, you were right," he whispered. "Some kind of government bullshit," he finished, spitting on the ground.

CHAPTER 12
THE CIRCUS

After they arrived Lucky and Kane sat around the table with Kanes mother and Grandpa. They told their stories. Grandpa smiled at them solemnly, and wondered how things had come full circle.

They did not know what to think when Grandpa said "Let me tell you more of the story about the time I joined the circus," but they listened intently as he started.

Lavinia sat by the fire. She had never wished for time to pass quickly before, but she really wanted next week to be here. They were heading back to Marion. It had been four years since she met Henry. The two boys that had come walking into camp on their grand adventure.

Henry went back to work on the farm, but every year, when they reached Marion, he would come out and work Marion with them, and then go on to the next town, but then always back to the farm. She resented the farm little but knew that he loved it and loved his family.

Greg had become quite the circus performer. Who knew that he would be so good on the trapeze? She remembered Greg telling her about Henry jumping for the train and the exhilaration of catching him. He said that he felt that way every night.

She had moved to the trapeze too. Her natural athleticism served her well. On Friday night she would do the fortune-telling, but over the years it seemed like more and more of the crowd had moved away from the ancient ways. She had even been invited to attend a birthday party for someone to tell the fortunes of everyone there. *It's for the best*, she thought. Some of her visions had been quite dark as of late.

They should have been in Marion by then, but they had added an extra stop. Derrick told her that it was good money, and the townspeople had been asking him to stop there for years. Lavinia actually argued with him. She could not tell him the reason for her not wanting to come to this place was the things the cards were showing her. "He would never believe," she said and spat into the fire.

"After tomorrow night we are done here, Lavinia," Derrick said. "See, I told you nothing would go wrong. Only issue we had was we lost that one stake."

She remembered and a chill caught her. She quickly agreed. "You are right," and looked into the fire for a sign, for warmth, and a sign of prosperity, but while she saw plenty of signs, none of them were good.

The stake went missing the first day. Larry had been driving in one of the stakes for the big top, and nearly broken his back on it. He'd been expecting it to be like the others he had started on. The soil here was hard as a rock. Swinging hard when the sledgehammer hit the stake, it had driven it deep into the ground and disappeared. Larry grabbed his back and cursed before yelling, "Sink hole, boss."

Derrick looked it over and decided for safety to move the tent a little. "We will stack the hay for the animals here, that way there are no seats near this, in case it gets wider. Put a board or two over it, Larry," he directed.

That was it. No one thought of the sink hole again. That is, except for Lavinia. She could think of nothing else. It haunted her dreams. She knew that something was there, and she prayed to all the spirits to protect them.

That night she dreamed she was on top of a stone pyramid. She was wearing bones and jewels around her neck and on her arms. She was wearing nothing else except for a beautiful black jaguar hide.

In her left hand she held a stone knife, one that had been her mother's, and her mother's mother before her, and as far back as any remembered.

In her right hand she held the still beating heart of one of their enemies. Turning, she held the heart out to the side of the pyramid. There was a hole there that was darker than the jaguar's fur. Darker than the darkest cave, and she could sense something coming. Holding her arm in the opening she called its name, saying the words that her ancestors all knew. Giving this enemy's heart to it and telling it that the others in the cages being lowered were an offering. The screams from the cages woke her.

"I am glad tonight is the last night," she said, reaching for her water pitcher, pouring some into a glass, and finished it before adding another.

Greg knocked on the side of the trailer. "Everything okay, Lavinia?" he asked. He shared the trailer beside hers with a few of the other men.

"Come in," she called, and once inside, she explained about her bad dream, one where she was feeding her enemy's heart to the shadows.

"Remind me to stay on your good side," he said, laughing. Then he added, "I just wanted to work on our routine a little today. Yesterday, I hurt my hand helping Larry. His back is still tender, and I wanted to be sure we were good to go. We can work with the net at first and remove it for the show if all is well."

Shaking off her dream, she promised to be out shortly if he would get her some coffee. Thinking back, she wondered why she did not pick Greg, but picked Henry, she knew the answer already because in the cards she read "Greg doesn't have a future" and she tried to shake that thought off as well.

The morning's practice went well, as did the afternoon show. Greg was so good, a natural. He told her many times how glad he was that they had found them. "It's fate," he said, and she knew it to be true.

One more show, then I'm safe with Henry. she thought and knew this was going to be when she stopped travelling. They were boys when she first met them. She only just turned eighteen, and they both fourteen, but last year she had become so close to Henry, and even though she was older than him, she knew he was feeling the same.

"I'll be your best man," Greg said, waking her up from her thought of last year with Henry.

"What?" she said, blushing. Not looking at him, she continued, "Thank you, Greg, you will be a great best man, if only you would shave that beard," she teased and then looking up at him, she almost screamed, "Let's run to Henry now," but she thought that it was just this place. "You shaved!" she exclaimed instead.

Greg chuckled and said "I have a date tonight after the show, and I figure I should clean up a bit. "He was about to go on when she interrupted him.

"A small blonde," she said.

"How did you know?" he asked and, not knowing what to say, Lavinia stood up and hugged him, harder than she meant to, saying, "I'll be back, have to check on something, don't start without me."

That was a common joke they had. Since it was a two-person act. Otherwise, he would be just up there swinging by himself. In her darkest visions, Greg was clean shaven and there was fire.

In the back of her trailer she found a grease pencil and in the small mirror, she drew as many protective symbols on her body as she could, remembering those on her body from the dream.

Dressing, she looked in the mirror, and the face looking back at her was that of the priestess.

"You look amazing, What did you do?" Greg asked when she reappeared.

"Bend down," she commanded, and he instantly obeyed. None of his usual jokes. She started drawing on his face.

"These will make you look great, now that you don't have that beard," she lied, trying to remain calm.

She had the symbols almost perfect when someone came walking up. Greg, turned his head and seeing the blonde, went to give her a hug and help her to her seat in the front row. As she watched him go, Lavinia was hopeful the protections would be enough.

Climbing up to the top of the trapeze felt so much easier than it had in the past; all the past days' nerves fell away. *Just being silly,* she thought as she prepared. Greg was already out, going back and forth, getting into position. She waved at the crowd, before swinging out, releasing her legs, and momentarily floating in the air, before grabbing his arms. The crowd clapped and cheered for them.

They did a few more tricks, both feeling the excitement of the night. Greg was so happy, and on one of the last aerial tricks, having time, he glanced down at his friend and winked at her.

He noticed at her feet a shadow moving. It did not appear to be moving with the light, but opposite it.

Lavinia saw where his eyes were and knew that he would look back and catch her. Doubt of that did not cross her mind, but then she saw it and screamed.

Hearing the scream, Greg looked back and grabs for her. He missed with the left, but his right was as sure as ever and makes it in time to keep her from falling. The same hand he had caught Henry with. "Something is down there!" he screamed to her, and he knew that she has seen it as well.

Getting back on the board, both stand as the crowd cheers and claps again. Derrick and Larry both wondered if they were going to add something new to the act as they saw them waving and pointing.

Larry, wearing stilts to make him even taller than he already was, saw what they were pointing at, but did not understand it was a shadow. For him he thought it was as snake and fear instinct took over. As he stepped backwards, his back spasmed and he tripped over someone, and went down to the ground. His hand caught one of the lanterns used to set the mood. They had electric lights and spotlights, but people still expected to see oil-filled lanterns. It fell to the ground, breaking as oil caught fire and splashed onto the side of the tent.

Larry's arm covered in oil quickly caught fire as his costume ignites. He rolled, trying to put out the fire, but ended up lighting the hay on fire.

The audience screamed as one. Lavinia could taste their fear, and with that she knew what drew the creature to the prisoners in her dream.

The creature moved up through the stands like a dark fog and as it touched the audience members, they screamed and aged as it devours their lives. Almost an entire town. She started to cry as she said, "They had no future."

"What?" Greg asked.

"Greg, they are all dead, we have to get out of here. We can help from outside. Climb up with me!" she begged, but already knowing that he would not go.

Looking down, he saw his blonde friend. She was standing in the center of the ring, screaming as the fire spreads over the canvas and the shadow devouring everyone around her.

"I have to try and save her if I can. She is only here because of me. If I don't make it, tell Henry I had the adventure of a lifetime and please thank him for me," he said as he started climbing down, yelling to his friend to try and climb up.

Lavinia, on the top of the trapeze, started to climb up the rope, climbing to the top of the big top, knowing that if she can reach the top, she knew she could make her way through the opening and slide down one of the sides not yet on fire.

Her last glance showed her Greg beside the blonde, a torch in his hand and fire in her hair. Just like her dream, he looked like what she imagined Hephaestus the blacksmith of the gods looked like with fire all around him as shadows danced in the flames.

She reached the ground and the sounds inside of the tent stopped. It was eerily quiet as she ran towards the cages and the corral for the horses. Being a good rider, she knew that on horseback that she may stand a chance and be able to get out of there. They are all dead she knew, and she must get to Henry. Then she would be safe.

Reaching the cages they were empty, she almost tripped on a small lamb she did not see. Stopping, she looked down at it.

The shadow was coming for her. She knew it. She did not have time. The shadow was hungry, it had been so long since she had last fed. The creature had been asleep for a very long time. Lavinia knew this. Just as she knew what to do to stop it.

Scooping up the lamb, she turned, and inside her head and aloud, she screamed the creature's name. Not any of the many names that it has been called over the years, but a name that was passed down for generations. She called the ancient name. She knew it as well as she knew her own name.

Perhaps it was something in her blood, perhaps it was that she was psychic, and dreams of the creatures invaded her own. She was not sure, but she knew what she had to do.

The creature, upon hearing its name, came for her, and it would devour her, taste her fear, and devour her, but there was no fear in this one. There was only the sacrifice. Lavinia, the high priestess, faced the shadow.

She named it and demanded of it to sleep. To accept this sacrifice and to sleep until called again.

Grandpa stopped talking, took a drink of water then added, "Kane, that was your Grandmother Liv. She shortened her name, so that she would fit in more with the neighbors. Some were a little prudish. Oh, but not yours Lucky," Grandpa Milner finished, winking at her.

Grandpa Milner continued, "I was just finishing supper when I heard something outside, opened up my door, and there she was, half naked on horseback. So tired she slept for a night and a day. I don't know how she found the farm. I had never told her the address, and later she told me that she just followed her heart," Grandpa said with tears in his eyes.

"Hearing the story, I believed her instantly and neither of us told anyone that she was at the circus that night. It was always just a tragic accident, and we did not want anyone asking questions about the town or the circus. She was afraid they may think she started the fire. My parents loved her, and a year later Kane, your mother was born. It's always the best ones that burn brightest and don't stay with us."

Lucky had not expected any of this when she started telling them of how her mom, uncle Ed and Joe had sacrificed themselves to kill the last creature. When Grandpa started telling his story, after Lucky leaned back into Kane's arms, the only place she felt safe, and said "I'm glad it is over. We can finally grieve."

"But you don't understand, Lucky," Grandpa said. "You killed the babies. Ed, Joe, and your Ma killed the dad, but Mama is so much larger, and I just hope she is still asleep."

He handed Lucky a journal. "You will marry Kane soon, so you are family. This is the birthright of women in our family. Your Grandmother would have loved her, Kane."

Grandpa moved to the living room, sat down, and appeared to go back inside himself as he picked up the remote, turned on the TV and, grinning, flipped to the all-day yoga channel.

AFTERWORD

It was two months before Sheriff Madagan called Lucky. Her cell had been left at the cabin, but she transferred the number to her new phone. The guy at the store had been funny.

"You want a phone that does not have GPS, and you want it to have a removable battery," he laughed and asked, "You are one of those aren't you? You are a lot more attractive than the usual tin-foil-hat-wearing people I see."

Kane had been in the Mustang during this exchange. He was doing better, but still felt it when it rained. The getting up and down process still hurt, and spending time on the tractor had reopened his wounds.

"Who knew Grandpa Milner could stitch someone up," she said after his grandpa had finished. Kane had been a little tipsy and feeling no pain. Alcohol was not the perfect painkiller, but it worked.

They spent time with Kane's family and, instead of heading back to college like she had planned, they decided to stay there for a while, to grieve and eventually take the Mustang to Mexico. She did not know how far their reach was and reading the journal she could tell Lavinia and Grandpa had travelled there a few times looking for answers.

She knew that her mother and father had left her more than she would ever need, and the same was true of Uncle Ed. With whatever it was, she could pay off all their debts so that Ma and Grandpa could live on the farm if they wanted without working so hard, or they could stay where they were if they decided. She just knew that they could not stay with them.

"Something is coming, Kane. I know it. I'm not sure how much time we have. I feel it searching for us," she told him late one night, and it was decided that they would go.

They checked on the news while staying with Kane's family, and Ginger's home was blamed as a gas line explosion. From the television she heard "The entire area is unstable." The story did not surprise Lucky. It was only when the camera crew panned back, and she saw the white SUVs that she'd been surprised. She turned it off when the broadcaster finished, "And no bodies were recovered."

This was the government! she thought. *Did they cause it, or were they trying to find it?* She did not know but she did sense that it was not over. She reached down and grabbed Kane's hand, holding it in hers. She saw the journal that Grandpa Milner had given her. Thoughts of this and the story he had told them were on both their minds as they drove into the morning sunshine.

When the sheriff called her, he was very formal. "Is this Janet Evans?" he asked, and immediately Lucky knew people must be listening.

"This is Janet," she answered back, confirming to Sheriff Madigan that she understood.

"I am sorry to inform you that your parents are not missing as you reported. They died in the explosion. Once it was determined they were there, I tried calling you at college but you must not be back there yet," he said, before going on to tell her how sorry he was and asking if she was at college. She said that she was not but had been and explained that she and her boyfriend were going to head to New York to check on some family.

She thanked him for his time and promised to come by his office and see him as soon as she returned from New York.

At the end, the sheriff went off the approved script and said "I've told the insurance companies about the deaths, and the death certificates have been filled out. Everything is good to go, and since they are a national agency, they said you could stop into any branch. The one by your college or in New York. They are sorry for your loss as well, and they will work with you."

Before she could say thank you, the phone went dead. Funny how it had seemed like the sheriff did not want to keep the line open for long, talking quicker than normal. Lucky realized he had done just that, to help her and help her with the funds. She flipped the phone over and removed the battery.

The money would help eventually, but thanks to Ed's paranoia they had plenty in the seats of the Mustang. It was Kane that discovered it. He was lying in the back complaining about how uncomfortable it was when he found the stash. They both laughed until they cried, seeing the money and a few guns that Uncle Ed had left. They packed up everything and started on their journey.

Hours into the trip, Lucky turned the music down, she looked over at Kane. How he could sleep with the top down she would never understand, thankfully he was resting up for whatever comes their way.

The only thing she had taken from her parents house was a rocking chair, her father and mother used to rock her in. She thought of this, and was glad she left it with Kane's mother and Grandpa.

"Lucky knew something was coming. She was not sure from where, but she knew, and you will never find her," the witness said to the man in white.

"Will you?" the man in white asks.

The witness looks up, wondering what that meant.

"COME ON. You don't get it? I know who you are," the man in white yelled at him.

"Of course, you do, we've been talking for months," the witness responded calmly.

Laughing, the man in white asked a flurry of questions. "And in all this time have you once left this room? Have you gone to the bathroom? Have you looked at what you are eating? Have you noticed all of the dust on the table from the rats you've been absorbing?"

The witness, shook with laughter, looked up and said, "You are trying to confuse me. I hit my head when the stairs collapsed. That's all. You've been interviewing me every day about what happened."

The man in white looked down at Ed, noticed his black eyes. He saw Ed smiling up at him. He could see the blackness behind his teeth, at the corner of his eyes, and remembered finding him in the flop house. He'd at first assumed he was drunk, or on drugs, not yet knowing that there was a creature in him. He'd thought to just sober him up and interview him. It must have been so small inside him at first. It had used up a lot of its own energy to bring Ed back to life, well a life of sorts.

How had he survived? How did this creature survive? He wanted to just kill it when he found out, but knew he had to find out as much as possible about them.

Ed scratched at his arms, and this time the man in white noticed that he could see the shadow swirling just below the skin in the scratch marks. The creature had almost used him all up, and was why it was trying to pretend to be Ed he did not know.

"I'll give you this," the man in white began as he exited the plastic room, securing it behind him. The Ed creature stood for the first time in months and walked over to the side of the plastic.

"What will you give me?" it asked as the man in white saw Ed's skin move with the shadows under.

"Ha, that is just what I'm talking about. You see, I've been interviewing you every day, and every time you've let a little more of the truth out. From what I knew about Ed, the first time you told the story, you said that Ed had made it to the top of the steps and ran away, abandoning his family. I did not know Ed personally, but I knew that could not be true. I have interviewed a lot of people and the only thing Ed cared about was family."

Reaching up to flip over the small sign above the button, he smiled as he read it to himself remembering a story his boss told him. He asked, "Do you know what this sign says?" while pointing to it.

"How would I know?" the creature asked.

"Thank you for that," said the man in white. "I wondered if you could read, and now we know. You have given me all you will. I know to keep you alive any longer would be foolish, and my boss is anything but foolish. He has been fighting your kind for a very long time," he said as the creature started to expand through and out of Ed in the small enclosure. Looking for any shadow, any crack, anything that could help it escape.

"If Ed is in there, tell him I'm sorry for making him stay around so long. I had to know as much as possible. Just so you know I will find and protect Lucky. I promise," he declared.

The guard who had always been curious about the sign read it aloud. "In Case of Emergency ROCK!" as the man in white pushed the button. Music starts and the lyrics "I think that someone is trying to kill me, infecting my blood, and destroying my mind..." the song from Mastodon Blood and Thunder pierces the room as the creature howls in pain and terror.

FROM THE AUTHOR

I'm David Musser and this is my first attempt at writing something of this magnitude. I hope that you have enjoyed Lucky's story. Who knows, maybe someday we will revisit Lucky and Kane? I do want to know more about them, and I hope that Grandpa keeps the TV off the workout channel. Most of all, I hope that the lights stay on.

I have started to work on the second novella and will post more on my website when I do at dmusser.com

I do find that music helps me concentrate as I write, so please check out my music list on the next page. Dyslexia go figure.

To learn more about David Musser and discover more Next Chapter authors, visit our website at www.nextchapter.pub.

MUSIC PLAYLIST

When writing I found that music helped me focus. I thought it would be good to include my playlist for anyone interested:

1. Devil – Shinedown
2. Feel Invincible – Skillet
3. Monster – Skillet
4. Basket Case – Green Day
5. Hero – Skillet
6. Ain't No Rest for the Wicked – Cage the Elephant
7. Straight to Hell – Ozzy Osbourne
8. Take What You Want (feat. Ozzy Osbourn & Travis Scott) – Post Malone
9. Blood and Thunder – Mastodon
10. Ordinary Man – Ozzy Osbourne
11. Hard To Forget – Sam Hunt
12. Enter Sandman – Metallica
13. Ghosts – Sugarhouse
14. Fake It – Seether
15. Seven Nation Army – The White Stripes
16. Natural – Imagine Dragons
17. Paranoid (2016 Remaster) – Black Sabbath

Keep In The Light
ISBN: 978-4-82419-037-6

Published by
Next Chapter
2-5-6 SANNO
SANNO BRIDGE
143-0023 Ota-Ku, Tokyo
+818035793528

28th January 2024